I0615462

Gentle Current

Into Danger

Books in The Looking Glass Saga:

LOOKING GLASS SAGA

BOOK EIGHT

Gentle Current Into Danger

TANYA LISLE

SCRAP PAPER ENTERTAINMENT

Copyright © 2020 by Tanya Lisle

All rights reserved. No part of this book may be reproduced
in any form by any electronic or mechanical means includ-
ing photocopying, recording, or information storage and
retrieval without permission in writing from the author.

ISBN-13: 978-1-988911-74-8

Scrap Paper Entertainment
www.scrappaperentertainment.com

Contents

CHAPTER 1

Deck the Halls

SLEEP ELUDED ALICE as her head continued to pound. She could pretend that the headaches weren't happening most of the time with enough Advil, but in the late hours of the night they kept her up and reminded her of everything she was missing. Instead of going to Wonderland, here she was, sitting in front of the mirror and staring back at her reflection in the darkness, considering what she should do with her life now.

Well, besides the obvious. There was no Wonderland for her to go to anymore. The mirrors wouldn't open for her, no matter how hard she looked. She was stuck on this side with a headache from trying to keep the madness from spilling over.

She hadn't noticed the madness until she got home. No one had mentioned that she was saying anything unusual or strange, but her father had caught on immediately. Thankfully, he thought that she was just being rebellious and quarantined her to the house. At least she was allowed out of her room. After all, she shouldn't be in her room all day when she could be doing the chores that the other women who used to inhabit this house once did. Without her mother or Ms. Miller, Alice was now in charge of keeping the place tidy.

The cameras were still on at all times, watching her every move during the day. Alice didn't know if her father was keeping an eye on the cameras at all times, but she learned from last time that she couldn't let herself get complacent. She was allowed to wander the house alone, though not permitted to leave or to access either her phone or the internet, though she was allowed her computer as she needed it for school. Her only allowed activities were chores, which she took her time with, and homework, which was difficult to do without any access to resources outside of the books in her house. And half of her textbooks were now merely textbook covers concealing fiction.

Given that, though, she had been able to finish her homework fairly quickly though not well. She was unable to cite sources for information she could include, unable to remember where she read things, unable to look it up. It was the best she could do to try and raise her low grades from the last semester, but that was not enough to raise them significantly. Her father didn't want to hear about it, blaming her for her low grades and insisting that she raise them if she wanted to have any freedom at all. She knew better than to argue.

She regretted finishing it early. She had no new books left on her shelves and she was scared to look at them too closely. Part of her feared to find that the real books would now be in those covers instead of those novels Ms. Miller had left her and that her father's ire had another reason behind it. Another part knew she had already read every book on her shelf, novel or not, and she would find no new escape there. Yet another part of her thought back to the stories, to the way the characters found their happiness at the end, and the knowledge that the happy ending for these characters was so often found in the arms of their true love left her feeling more isolated than comforted.

Alice got to her feet and went to her window, watching the dark of morning and wondering just what time it was. She had gotten so used to checking her phone during school that it was strange not to have it, though she was adjusting. She had to, after all. She was not allowed to use it, not for a very long time. Not until she was back in school.

She could hear the ticking of the clock in her room. It didn't have a backlight so she could see the time.

She did wonder how everyone else was doing. She couldn't see into Wonderland, and Cat didn't come here to taunt her about her imprisonment. She would have welcomed seeing him in the chrome sink while she was washing dishes. Or just about anywhere else. She was lonely and unable to concentrate most days. She wanted to talk to Adrianna or anyone else, and she would be willing to talk to anyone right now. The Mad Hatter could come in here and tell her how rude she was and she would welcome the company.

Taking a breath, she went to her laptop and opened the lid, looking at the internet icon and wondering. She didn't know the password for the house's wifi, so she would be unable to get access. Lance had been able to figure it out, but Alice didn't know how to do anything like that. There were a few things she could do on here, but all she did was look over the homework again and again. It was terrible. But it was all she could do.

She went back into the bookshelf that she had filled with her textbooks and let her finger run over them. She would not be able to go back to sleep now, and sitting in the dark staring at the computer was useless. Some of these books were actually text books, but she had long ago memorized every fact and figure in them and they bored her now. Maybe she could go back to a book she knew wouldn't make her feel too alone. One that ended well before anyone fell in love.

Her finger stopped briefly on *Harry Potter*. Maybe. The first book stopped well before any of that...

If only she could sleep. She was too tired, but not sleepy

enough to let the darkness take her again. She was just exhausted and desperate to get out, her head throbbing and miserably lonely like she never thought she could be.

"Just because you see no one does not mean there is no one there to see you," she mumbled to herself, quiet enough that if her father walked in he wouldn't have heard her. Sometimes when she spoke for a while, the headache would subside. If she stopped trying so hard to hold back the madness. "But if the other person is present and does not show themselves, then it is most rude and possibly offensive. Though perhaps speaking to the darkness is better than not speaking at all. Perhaps the darkness is as lonely as I am. Though you do not speak back, and that is terribly rude of you. You know how alone I am and even you will leave me."

She could feel tears stinging her eyes and she pushed that thought back. Best not to think that way. She was only going to depress herself doing that, and her father insisted that she had nothing to be sad about. It was her own fault that she had gotten herself grounded. If her grades hadn't been so bad, she would not have been in this situation. And this time she was allowed the run of most of the house, and even the television, so there was nothing for her to be upset by.

If she could just focus on her schoolwork and not be so caught up in Wonderland, she might be able to have full freedom, whatever that looked like. Access to the television while her father wasn't there, even if he did insist that he would know whatever she chose to watch, was still more than she was used to. The channels were mostly blocked, so she ended up putting on some mind numbingly dull shows about people making changes to houses or yelling about food, shows that her friends thought were trashy fun. She wished she could ask them now which ones would be good to actually pay attention to.

Her room gradually grew lighter and she could hear the door downstairs open and close. Her father had left for the day without even coming in and saying hello. Alice took this as a relief and it stayed that way as she went around the house for the day, doing chores and trying to pass the time. Outside, the rain was coming down in Washington and it never quite stopped being grey, leaving her stuck in a dull haze. She settled on a show where people were angry for her background noise. Someone in this house should feel something, even if it wasn't her.

She wanted to go back to school and to people. If she couldn't be in Wonderland, she hoped she could at least talk to someone again. If she hadn't ruined every friendship that she had yet. Somehow, she hoped that they still wanted to talk to her at least a little bit of the time. She had gone through the days wondering what she could possibly say to any of them to try and make any of them be friends with her.

Adrianna just seemed so worried about her. In the back of her mind, she kept trying to figure out the best way to make sure that she wouldn't be so worried anymore. She could just stop talking about Wonderland, she supposed. Try to keep that to a bare minimum. Make it a secret that she kept only for herself so that Adrianna didn't have to get so involved anymore.

But she hadn't asked her to get involved. Adrianna seemed mad when she didn't tell her about what was going on, but she was also not happy when she *did* know what was going on. Adrianna wanted it to be done and over, for Alice to move on with her life. And Alice wasn't thinking nearly that far ahead. She didn't know what was waiting for her after Wonderland, had no idea what she should expect. She was supposed to go to school, to get a job, to find a husband and have kids and settle down. That was what you were supposed to do in life, so that's what she would do. It didn't matter if Wonderland was there or not.

Except that Wonderland was getting in the way of school. And that was the bad part. That was the thing that she needed to resolve. That whole part about Wonderland interfering with her studies, that was what she was supposed to stop. So that she could do all of that. And pass her time, one day at a time.

Again, Alice's mind wandered back to how it was supposed to be. How she wasn't supposed to be here at all. She was supposed to lose. None of this was supposed to be her problem anymore. For all she had been told that being a statue was a terrible fate, she couldn't imagine it was much different than this. Except if she was a statue, no one would expect her to do anything. She wouldn't have to figure out how to make all these people happy.

She waited for the feeling to pass, scrubbing at the sink.

"You've made your own cage, Alice," she told herself absently. "You could walk away."

And she could, but she didn't know where she would go. Like Harry, she didn't have any place to go other than this house. She didn't know where other people lived, not really. Sarah was in California, but she didn't know where. She wasn't sure where Kevin's family was. Robert was in... Ohio? And Adrianna was out in New York, which was probably too far. Even if she wanted to go see Ms. Miller, she didn't know where her house was. She could break out of the house and call her, but she had no idea where she could go to find a phone. She had no way to call her and she had no way to get there. And Ms. Miller had probably moved on with her life. She'd probably forgotten completely about Alice and was working with other children now.

She stayed here because there was nowhere else for her to go. She wanted to leave, but there was no first step for her to take. She was stuck here. Forever. Or until she got into University. If she did. And then found a husband who would get her out of here for longer, only to keep her in a different house that she would be expected to keep.

It was only going to make her sad thinking about it. Escape was still a long way off and thinking about even being back in school was giving her hope that only made her far more tired. It made the wait feel even longer. Hope was the miracle that added more hours to an already long day and she could barely stand the hours dragging as it was. Not to mention the fear that one wrong move made in hope and in letting the headaches get the better of her might mean she spoke out of turn and said something strange. If she did, she could have her tuition to school withdrawn at her father's whim and she was not going to risk it.

The front door closed and she looked up, finding that she was in the middle of making dinner when her father got home. She barely knew what time it was or what had happened during the day, but it seemed that her body had performed all the tasks she was meant to do. She took a breath and prepared herself for her hour and a half of interaction with her father, wondering how much attention he would pay to her this time. Maybe he would ignore her entirely. Maybe he would actually speak to her. She hoped it was the former.

"Alice!"

It would be the latter tonight. That was unfortunate. Some days he wouldn't come home at all and the days would bleed into one another. The days already did that, but she wasn't sure if this was better or worse than the monotony and loneliness. Of the inability to sleep from the headaches and the days spent drifting through her existence.

"Hello," she said, coming into the room. "Dinner is almost ready."

"Good," he said. "We need to talk."

Alice was preparing herself for a talk as she brought out dinner. Her father sat himself at the head of the table and Alice took her spot to the side, letting him lead the way for the evening. She would do whatever she was asked so long as she was allowed to leave unscathed, and she didn't know if she would be able to do even that. Still, she would listen and not interrupt. "Yes, father?"

"*Father?*"

Already she'd crossed a line. He frowned at her, a sound emitting from his throat that sounded like he was taking away her tuition.

"Dad," she corrected herself.

"Why haven't you decorated?" he asked. "It's almost Christmas. Don't you think you should have put up something for it? I know that mother of yours usually did it, but she's not here anymore. I'm expecting you to keep up."

There was an edge, a bite whenever he talked about her mother. Alice nodded, understanding that she was supposed to pick up where her mother wasn't doing anything anymore now that she no longer lived here. She looked at the food in front of her, finding that she still wasn't hungry. She would nibble tonight and save this all for tomorrow. She didn't remember eating today, but she must have.

"I don't know where we keep any of the Christmas stuff," Alice told him. She also didn't know if they were going to bother this year. Her father hadn't been interested in it at all until this moment and seemed to have no inclination that he would want anything to do with the holiday beyond Mass. She was now stuck going to church every Sunday and still didn't know what was going on, but her father seemed very important there.

"Find it," he told her. "I'm getting a tree."

Alice nodded and looked down at her plate. "I will," she said obediently, turning her mind over with the thoughts. At least it would be something else to do. She could take that as a consolation, at least, where the rest of her day was just passing without any other note.

"You're not going to ask why?"

"Why?" she asked automatically. Best not to do anything that might cause an argument.

"Honestly, Alice, try not to look like I'm torturing you

in here," he told her sharply. "No one wants to be around someone who looks miserable all the time. We'll be having company for dinner this weekend. Your friend will probably be coming as well."

"Oh," she said. Clearly he wanted her to say something more. "That will be nice."

He let out a noise but went back to silence. Alice went back to nibbling until he left the table, leaving her to clean up. At least she would have something else to do while she was passing the time for a day or two. She didn't know who this friend was. She didn't know why any of them would willingly come to visit her. She wondered if he would tell her who it was. She didn't think he would like it if she asked. It might be too many questions.

She also would not let herself get excited over it. She knew what terrible things happened when she got excited or hopeful. Everything could be taken away at any time, so she would not start to try hoping for anything. Instead, she would try to find the decorations and decorate the tree when it showed up. She wondered if that meant there would be presents appearing under the tree. She wondered if they would be real. She wondered if she would get anything from her mother or from Lori.

She knew better than to wonder any of those things. All of that sounded too much like hope, and she pushed them all back down. She wasn't even sure what day it was now, so she had no idea how long she had until the weekend to get things together. She would need to spend tomorrow looking for decorations. At least there would be that to break the monotony of her days.

CHAPTER 2

Calling Reinforcements

THE SNOW OUTSIDE and the festive spirit inside should have had Adrianna in a good mood, but there was something missing from the holidays. The door across the hall from hers was slightly ajar and the room inside vacant this Christmas. She didn't like it one bit. Alice had become a staple of the holiday for her and she found her absence to be a detraction from the cheer around the rest of the house. Instead, she worried about the lack of any communication from her since school got out.

"She doesn't get to keep her phone, you know," Rayne told her. She sat on Adrianna's bed, watching her fret and stare at her phone like it would tell her something. "She'll be completely isolated in there. No people getting in to talk to her and tell her that this is messed up. Probably doesn't even get to keep her computer."

Adrianna wondered if she would just go into Wonderland, but she had always been more careful in her own house than at the Case's. Alice feared her father in a way that she could never quite admit to herself, terrified that the man would know that she wasn't normal and fearing what his wrath might mean. Adrianna wished he didn't get custody, but it had been a condition of her continuing to go to school. It didn't seem to her like he even wanted Alice around.

"Can't she just come here for the holidays?" Adrianna asked. "We could ask your dad directly, right? And maybe he'll let her come out here."

Rayne shook her head. "Then she'd be too close to Mom," Rayne said. "Mom would be happy to see her. And dad would not want that. If mom had gone to Texas, you might have a shot. I don't know what he's doing with her now. Probably just making her cook and clean and do whatever mom and Ms. Miller used to do."

"Ms. Miller?" Adrianna asked, confused and suddenly alert. That was the woman who used to keep an eye on Alice, who Lance said made sure Alice got food and didn't suffer too much. Who would give her books smuggled in with the wrong covers. That she was doing things that Alice needed to stay alive and sane, like take her out of the house and make sure she wasn't trapped in her room the whole time. "What happened to her?"

Rayne shook her head, scratching at her head of short blue hair and looking like she didn't like the words about to come out of her mouth. "She basically worked for Mom," Rayne told her. "Without Mom there, Dad stopped paying her. And if no one's paying her, you know, she won't keep working. Dad fired her, basically, and Alice is pretty much on her own over there. Unless you have any ideas."

"One," Adrianna said, looking down at her phone. "She said she'd get back to me as soon as she knew."

Rayne was interested now, looking at her and the phone. "It's not something illegal, is it?" she asked, though she looked like she would actually be completely fine with it if it were. "Which brother is involved in this?"

"None of them," she said, looking up to the shadow and footsteps coming for her door. "Yet."

"Hey, Addie," Lance said, leaning into the door. He spotted Rayne and stopped for only a second before that look came across his face. "Is this a being sad about Alice not being here meeting?" he asked, looking between the two.

"Apparently Addie has a plan."

"It's not to get her here," Adrianna clarified as soon as her brother turned that look on her, that look that was both parts skeptical that she knew what she was doing and concerned that if he heard anything about this plan, he would be implicated in the fallout when it went wrong. "I'm just getting someone to go there and check on her. Hopefully."

"I don't think her dad would like that much."

"It's not the cops or anything," Adrianna said. Although she would have liked to call the cops, Rayne was insistent that calling child services would get them nowhere. "But she might be able to…"

Her phone buzzed and dinged in her hand and she went right to it. Sarah finally got back to her. Finally. It was only a text to ask if she could just call, so Adrianna waved for them all to shut up and dialed.

"Hey, what happened?" Adrianna asked, almost breathless and the words all ran into each other as soon as she heard the call connect.

"Say hi first, Addie," Sarah said, laughing. "My break's going not too bad, how about you?"

"Hi Sarah."

"I'm putting up with my aunt for this," Sarah said. "I want this on record. In case Kevin ever tries to say I don't do anything for anyone again, you remind him of this. I'll see if I can get her to New Year's too."

"Let me know how she is?"

"That's the whole point of this," Sarah told her. "Don't worry, I'm sure she's fine. Even if that house is creepy as fuck. How are you doing? Brothers gone nuts yet? See Arthur?"

"No Arthur yet," she said, looking at Lance. He rolled his eyes, looking irritated by the mention of the name, but said nothing as she went back to the phone. "Still time, though. He's not trying to come to New Year's at least."

"Absolutely not invited," Sarah said. "I get a bad vibe from him. Why are you so interested, though?"

"I'll tell you about it later," Adrianna told her. "It has to do with... stuff."

"Ah, okay. I'll let you get back to your vacation. I'll give you a call as soon as I know anything."

"Thanks. Bye Sarah."

She looked back at the two pairs of eyes staring back at her, pleased with herself. "Apparently Sarah's aunt is dating your dad now. Sarah says she's a gold digger and she hates her, but she's tagging along to see Alice."

"So long as she's young and hot, Dad will go for her," Rayne said, looking at her own phone. "But she'll check on Alice and report back?"

Adrianna nodded. "Sarah will know."

"Good, because Jenn wants to meet up. Will you guys be okay without me for a few hours?"

"What did we need you for again?" Lance asked, smiling.

Rayne laughed, knocking lightly into him before getting out of there. Lance leaned into the doorway and shook his head as he looked her over. "Have I told you how stupid it was to make any kind of deal with Arthur?"

"It's just a date," Adrianna said.

"It was stupid," Lance said. "Still is."

"Like getting yourself possessed?"

"*Getting myself possessed,*" he laughed, hollowly and humorlessly. "Yes, this is exactly what I wanted. Possessed by Arthur's old best buddy who died years ago. Apparently good old Lancelot doesn't want to be here any more than I do."

"We'll figure out how to get you free of him too."

Lance shook his head, not coming any more in the room as he glanced back into the hall. He didn't lower his voice, which told Adrianna only one of two people could be coming down the hall. "I think he's staying for a reason," Lance said. "I get the feeling that if he really wanted to go, he would. And that he's letting me take the reins as often as he can."

"He shouldn't be there in the first place," Adrianna told him, frowning. "You're picking up bad habits from Alice. She keeps accepting things instead of trying to make them better for herself too."

"Are we shit-talking Alice?" Adam said, looking at Adrianna with far too cutting a grin. "Because I have a few things to add."

"No," Adrianna told him sharply. "I don't know what your problem with her is."

"I do," Lance said, groaning. "I've heard this before. I'm out. We have food downstairs when you're done listening." Lance ducked out and left before Adam could pull him into whatever he had to say. He spoke and his words fell behind his brother's, quiet in the background and then fading away entirely.

"She needs to get her shit together," Adam said. "If she actually stayed over there then she might actually get Wonderland back in order without having all this coming down around her. It's her responsibility, not mine, but I was at least willing to do something about it. And now where is she?"

"Trapped in her house?"

Adam shook his head. "She could just be in Wonderland and fixing things. What else does she have to do right now? Be grounded?"

"Not everyone wants to be in trouble," Adrianna pointed out. "Not everyone is you. She can't just give up everything and be fine with that. That's not how that works."

Adam wasn't moved. "Wonderland needs to be saved and she's the only one who can do it. I was willing to take it over, but she kept me from it and she won't even step in. And now look at what's happening. Tiger Lily's basically risking her life in her place instead and she's not even putting the hearts back."

"Maybe we should get dinner," Adrianna suggested. She

didn't like what Adam was going for now, how vindictive and mean he was becoming the more he was kept away from Wonderland. "What happened to you in there?" she asked as she pulled him along on the hall and down to the food downstairs. "You want to be back so bad, but why? What did they do for you in there?"

"It's what's right," he said. There was something strange in his eyes, something a little glassy despite the determination behind his words. "It's a whole world that needs to be saved. At any cost."

"You nearly killed someone to do it," Adrianna said.

That made him hesitate. "I never tried to kill anyone who didn't deserve it," he said. He knew well enough that he had tried to kill someone. At least, he knew that she would never believe that he hadn't tried to kill something given he had come out of Wonderland armed to the teeth and having fought and fought against the Queen of Hearts for so long.

"Arthur," Adrianna said. From his words, Adrianna wondered how many others there might have been.

"He deserved it," Adam told her, though he looked almost bewildered about the accusation. "He decided to assault my little sister while she was unconscious. And then she decided to agree to a date with him."

"Not about me," Adrianna told him, words sharp and

quick. "You tried to sacrifice him to a monster to save Wonderland."

"And that would have been fine. No one knew who he was. He was just going around and stalking people for a while. And then what does he do in the end? Nothing. No one would have known who he was. No one would have missed him. Like he never existed. It would have been fine if he just went away forever. No one would have caught anything. But Alice had to go and stop me."

"It's good that she did."

"She was willing to let herself get taken if she got to continue doing nothing," Adam snapped back at her. "She was willing to leave Wonderland high and dry, abandon it! She doesn't deserve to be its savior. At least I was trying to do something. And she wouldn't even let me do that. She'll just let it all go away and for what? Now we're stuck with nothing. Wonderland's screwed and she's not even going to go over."

Adrianna frowned. She didn't like how Wonderland was infecting the people around her and how terrible it was making her brother and her best friend. How alienating it was turning everything. Adam needed something else to distract himself and help him move on. Or maybe he just needed closure.

"And what happens if she doesn't save it all?" Adrianna asked. "What then? What if she walks away from it all? Nothing happens to your life. You still have to go ahead and live your life, finish school, go to college. You'll have enough to do. You should have more than enough to worry about already. You're a year behind now. You could be trying harder to try and make that up instead of trying to save a world that no one else even knows about."

"You say that like it doesn't matter."

Adrianna stayed quiet for the moment, not wanting to start on that argument again just yet. She didn't know how to navigate it yet. It wasn't real, though, not for much longer. Eventually it would leave Adam like it had left Alice before. And once it was gone, he would have to return to his life. If it kept lingering in his memories, he would remain trapped in the past. That was what had happened to Alice. Lingering in her memories threatened to ruin her chances of a future. And it was happening again.

"Tiger Lily could be brought out," Adrianna suggested. She saw him shift at that, see him consider and perk up. "You keep mentioning her. You like her, don't you? More than Heather."

"It's not about Tiger Lily," he insisted, though Adrianna wondered if that was a lie. Not entirely, but he was certainly fond of her. But she wouldn't come out on her own. Adam would have to go back in there if he wanted to be with her. So maybe, just maybe, she could help direct him to move on.

After all, he would be left here on this side eventually. And she would be over there. And they couldn't be together.

Adrianna said nothing else and they went to dinner, Adrianna letting her mind circle. She needed to disentangle her loved ones from Wonderland and she would. She just needed time to think about it and she could absolutely come up with a way of doing that.

CHAPTER 3

A Forced Christmas

IT TOOK A while to figure out where her mother had left all of the Christmas decorations, but Alice did manage to find them after a few hours and spent the rest of the day trying to replicate something that looked somewhat festive. She got out the ladder so she could hang garlands high enough that they framed the windows and tried to make it look nice around the living room and entry.

But she used it to pass the day. She could feel the length of the hours as they passed today, stretching on and not nearly filled enough as she nibbled at her dinner from the night before. She worked to put things up around the house. She didn't get it all up, given that it had taken her the better part of the day to find the decorations, and her father was upset that she didn't manage to do it faster or with better precision.

It took her another day to get the house fully decorated

to his standards when he finally brought in the tree for her to tend to. She had no internet to look up how she was supposed to take care of a Christmas tree, so she did her best to guess and read what she could from the books in the house. When nothing was available, she just did the best she could with what she had and managed to get the tinsel and lights onto it before her father got home.

He complained about the fallen needles, but had little else to draw his ire at the moment. Alice considered it a success, but also knew that there was something hollow about this victory. She had been working all day and found that the hard work made the day pass faster at least, though it also made her realize how much longer she had before she would be allowed to leave again. The break in the monotony was making things worse rather than better. The days until she went back to school seemed far too many now and they stretched before her like an impossible journey.

More and more, she was staring longingly at any reflective surface around her, hoping for some kind of escape. She wanted to go to Wonderland so badly, where time didn't have so much of a hold on her and where there were at least things to do. There was something to this monotony that was so torturous. To the knowledge that as soon as this weekend passed, she was going to have to go right back to doing nothing all day but cook and clean. To laundry that didn't need to be done that regularly. To television shows that passed by in the background. To the same books over and over again that promised her a break so long as she never told a soul that they existed. At least, so long as her father never learned that she was reading them.

She tried not to think too much about what was coming, but she couldn't help herself. The monotony was broken and her mind was engaged again, thinking about what was coming and realizing time was passing again. He said one of her friends was coming, but she had not dared to ask him which one it was yet. She didn't want to ask, too concerned that the question might have unintended consequences. That he might be mad that she was trying to find out if this was really a friend or someone else entirely.

Or if they would decide not to come. She didn't want to get excited about company only to have that hope ripped so quickly away and she would be trapped here in the silence again. She didn't want to risk a thing like that, only to sink into a depression she could now recognize as a bad thing. She wanted to have the time pass and save her excitement for school, to do nothing that would risk that eventual goal. She would need to be careful with her friend there, if it was a friend, and she would need to continue being a model child if she wanted to be allowed to go back again. That was the deal.

When Saturday rolled around, her father was more matter of fact about it than anything. Alice got ready and looked nice, though wore an apron for most of the day and spent it in the kitchen. He wanted a home-cooked meal, something adequately Christmas-like without it being over the top. He had settled on ham and several other fixings and instructed Alice to make it all. She would be doted on as a good cook, she knew, and she was prepared for it. She still didn't know who was coming. He said it was a girlfriend, a woman who would be a much better woman than her mother. Alice said nothing in response, barely listening and agreeing where she needed to. She just wanted the night to be over with so she could continue to drift through time until she could go back to school.

She heard the door open and her father greeted a woman at it. She sounded like the women on the television shows and Alice barely paid any attention, even as she heard that someone was being sent in her direction. She didn't look up from cooking, knowing that she would be called when it was time to be seen, but she had not expected her father to really want her to be there with his girlfriend.

"Alice?" came a voice behind her. She knew that voice. "Hey, you're still alive!"

Alice looked up from her cooking and turned back around, her face staying blank and tired as she looked at her. Sarah was standing there on the other side of the counter, coming around and getting closer and closer, arms out and clearly ready to embrace her. She didn't know what to make of it at first, barely registering it was happening until Sarah snatched the spatula out of her hand and gave her a hug.

"Hey," Alice said, getting herself together at least enough to reciprocate the hug. She was supposed to do something here. She knew she was, but she couldn't quite remember what. She hadn't thought it would be someone she actually knew. She didn't know what she was expecting, but Sarah had not been it. "How are you?"

"Better than you from the look of it," she said, pulling back and looking her over. "No one's heard from you at all since we got home. You can't just go silent because it's the holidays. We thought you were dead and buried in the backyard or something." She looked her over again and frowned, peering at her face. "You aren't sleeping, are you?"

Alice knew she was being carefully studied from the way Sarah was looking at her, like she was watching for something specific in her appearance. She backed away, startled that Sarah was actually there and watching her so closely. Alice was suddenly very aware of what she must look like, nice though she was, and that her face was not portraying what it needed to. She was supposed to be smiling. Happy. Greeting guests and ready to be hospitable.

Alice put the smile in place and tried to straighten up,

fumbling with the apron and turning off the elements on the stove. "I'm fine," she said, coming back to herself and understanding what was happening. She took her hair out of her ponytail and tried to adjust a headband that wasn't there. She hoped her father would consider this presentable enough. "Did you have to come a long way? Don't you live in California?"

Sarah shook her head, a tight smile stretching across her lips. "I'm visiting the family," Sarah said with a wink. "On request. Putting up with my slut of an aunt for you. We've been worried, Alice. And you have definitely not been sleeping. Does he let you out at all?"

Alice smiled and shook her head dismissively. "I'm grounded," she said. "My grades suck."

"You aren't responding to even email."

"No phone, no internet," Alice said. "But I get television now, so it's not that bad. So long as I can get my grades back up, I should be able to get my phone back next summer."

"No *internet* should be a crime," Sarah said, pulling herself up onto the counter and watching her. She picked up a spatula and smacked Alice's hand with it when she tried to go back to cooking. "And you've been cooking all day for us?"

"Do you like ham?" Alice asked. "I don't think I actually know."

Sarah smacked her hand lightly as she went back to tend

to the food again. "Alice," she said. "You look terrible. What's been going on?"

"Nothing," she said.

"Alice."

The stare Sarah gave her made her stop. She was trying to figure out where she was right now, if she should be spending the time trying to decide whether or not to be like her father wanted her to be or as she was in school because Sarah was here. She knew there were cameras watching, but her father was likely too busy to be monitoring them right now. And in this moment, Sarah was staring at her like she wanted answers and like she wasn't going to leave until she got them.

"I am putting up with my aunt for you. The least you can do is be honest with me."

"Nothing," Alice said. "Nothing has been going on. At all."

"You're lying, Alice."

"I'm really not," she said. She glanced back at the door to make sure there was no one about to come around the corner, but she was in no danger of that. Her dad and the other woman was over in another room far from them, laughing and opening what sounded like a bottle of wine. She lowered her voice to continue. "I haven't left the house. I'm not allowed to go anywhere. I've just been here, doing homework and chores the whole break."

Sarah looked at her carefully. "And not sleeping."

"I've had headaches," Alice said. "Still have headaches. It's fine."

Sarah let out a deep sigh and looked like she didn't know what to do with Alice. "Look, here's the plan," she said. "We're going to let my aunt distract your dad. And then we're going to get your dad to agree to let you come see me for New Year's down in Cali. And when we're done, you are going to say thank you and we are going to get you out of here and you can tell me what's actually going on."

Alice nodded. "Okay."

"Okay?" Sarah looked almost offended.

"I'm sorry."

"For what?" Sarah asked. She looked like she was about to say something else, to get mad, but she kept it back. "You look like you didn't even know I was going to be here, Alice."

"I didn't."

"What?"

"He didn't tell me who was coming," Alice said. "A few days ago, he just said I needed to decorate for Christmas and that there was going to be company. I didn't know who was going to be here."

Sarah nodded again. She still looked like she wanted to say something, but she pulled Alice away from the kitchen instead and started to bring her further into the house. "Hey,

Rachel, I'm taking Alice and doing her makeup, okay?" she called into the house.

"Whatever you girls want!" her aunt yelled back, giggling between sounds of clattering glass. Sarah led them past the pair and Alice could see her father was quite preoccupied with the woman in the tight black dress and a lot of makeup. Sarah made a sour face as they went past, but didn't say anything until they got to the stairs. Alice led her up to her room, to the strange lock on her door and to the bathroom where she could work.

"Your house is so creepy," Sarah said, taking a makeup pallet out of her purse and setting the instruments out across the table. It wasn't the first time she had said it, but Alice still wasn't sure what she was supposed to do about it.

"Dad's just—"

"This is not about security," Sarah told her firmly as she started to work on Alice's face. "You are lying to me and I'm going to keep putting stuff on your face until you tell me the truth. You can lie to Addie all you want, but you don't get to do that to me."

Alice said nothing, not sure what was going on here and not much liking it, but she was trapped already. She let Sarah start working on foundation that covered the lines and dark circles under her eyes, cover the pimples from stress and lack of proper hygiene, cover the lines of worry and fill the blank feeling that she had been feeling the whole time she had been home with… something.

"I've been talking to some people," she said. "Other people who were in that forest with me. They tell me you saved them from the Bandersnatch and that he wasn't going to let you out of it before. That you went there not to save yourself but to save that asshole, Arthur."

Alice didn't say anything, her eyes staring back at the door. She couldn't hear how far away her father was, but she hoped that it was far enough that she wouldn't have to explain this conversation. He didn't have any cameras in her room, but he could walk in at any moment.

Not only that, she needed to remember how to respond like a human. Sarah was expecting something from her and she was not giving her anything.

She needed to snap out of it, but her facades and feeling of nothingness ran much too deep and she couldn't remember how emotions worked. She wasn't sure she wanted to let them back in. Sarah was only here for a little while. Soon she would be gone and Alice would be left alone again. Back to the monotony of nothing for the next couple weeks until she was allowed back to Lucena Academy.

If she was allowed.

"Well?" Sarah pressed.

Alice shrugged. She was stuck. "What?" she asked. "I

didn't know how to get out of it. I didn't think I could come up with anything."

"They were all going to be trapped in there forever."

Alice nodded. "Someone else might have been able to save them."

"You were going to be in there with them. Forever."

Alice said nothing. She still wondered what that would have been like. If it were like this existence now. If that's what it was. Just standing there, staring out at nothing like that and waiting for life to happen around her. If there was nothingness like what she was feeling now. This same emptiness that she was waiting to pass. If it was perhaps better because there would be no end to it and no one trying to make her do anything.

Sarah started to say something. "Don't tell me..." she started, but she didn't seem to want the answer to whatever she was about to ask. "Fine, but you got them all out in the end. Which is good. But you need to be more careful. You know that he'll keep you in there forever if he can."

Alice agreed, but she couldn't move with the way Sarah's hand was keeping her face still. She could speak, but she had nothing else that she could say about the matter right now. "He's gone now," Alice said.

"He is," Sarah agreed. If anyone could feel that he was gone, it would be Sarah. Which was good for Alice, at least.

"But you're reckless. And that's why you're going to be more careful next year, right? And from now on?" She started working on Alice's lips to keep her quiet and prevent her from arguing. "You need to stop trying to get yourself in so much trouble and instead start trying to keep yourself safe so that you can get out of these things and survive to the next. And I don't care how hopeless it seems, you don't get to give up. Got it? Now, what else is going on?"

She let go of Alice's chin and left her lips alone while she went back to her kit. Alice watched her, trying to figure out what she was talking about. "What do you mean?"

Sarah glared at her, withholding something in her hand that Alice recognized as eyeliner. "I swear to God, Alice, I will jam this right in your eye if you try to tell me that there's nothing happening again," she said, coming at Alice with the eyeliner. "We're going to do this nice and carefully until you actually tell me everything. And maybe a little longer so I don't have to talk to Rachel again."

Alice frowned and didn't know what else to say to her. "I really don't know—"

"Yeah, none of that," Sarah told her. "You look like you've had the life drained out of you and like you've lost a shit ton of weight. Are you eating? You aren't sleeping. You're swimming in that dress. And you look like shit, no matter how much you might clean up. And you keep looking at the mirror like it's going to do something for you, which it absolutely is not." She paused, frowning as she let the pen drag a little further along her eyelid. "But it used to, didn't it? Last year, every time you were around the mirrors would always do weird stuff. Rob was mentioning that."

Sarah narrowed her eyes on her, though that may have had more to do with the eyeliner. "The Bandersnatch said something about Wonderland before too, right? And I've seen you fall through the floor into some other world. What was that place? What was all that about?"

"Nothing," Alice said.

"Ah, so that's it," Sarah said. "Adrianna mentioned something about Wonderland too. I'm thinking that's what this is all about. That's where you had to send the Bandersnatch. What is that place and what's it to you?"

"It doesn't matter," Alice told her. Like it had happened before with Adrianna, she could feel herself ready to burst with it all and let it out in a stream, whether or not she wanted it to. "I can't go back now anyway. They won't let me come back now. So I have to stay here. I can't go back and they covered everything on their side so I can't get across. There's weather, so I can't even get through on the lakes. So I'm stuck on this side and it doesn't matter anymore what happens."

She could feel herself starting to cry and sucked in a

deep breath, returning to that blank monotony as much as she could. She started to speak again, Sarah pulling back her brush and watching as she put her walls right back up. She didn't look happy about it, but Alice knew what she had to do to make it through this break.

"I need to focus on my life here now," she said, remembering what Adrianna wanted. It's what her father wanted. It's what was expected of her. "I'm not going to be able to go back again, so I need to pay attention to my life here now. Go back to school. Get married. Have kids. All that stuff."

A pang went through her and more spilled out as her head throbbed.

"It is the only proper thing for a proper young woman," Alice added. "And a proper young woman is what I will be, as it's expected. But underneath I will know it is only a costume and I will never be truly happy. But being an adult is not so much about being happy as it is about learning which lines you are never allowed to cross and to never again cross them, no matter how much your heart may want to."

Sarah froze, eyes widening and watching Alice carefully. She didn't move, like she was scared Alice would run if she moved too much.

Alice felt something strange and realized what had happened almost too quickly. In the mirror, she could see the shock on her face evident in her eyes widening. She sealed her mouth shut, eyes darting around in fear that she was over-heard.

"No one's listening," she said gently, glancing over her shoulder to the closed washroom door. She clearly didn't know what was going on, but Alice resettled herself.

Alice looked straight ahead at the door where there was no one and sat up a little straighter, her breathing shallow and forced to be even as she made her shoulders stay where they should be. She was going to be proper and she was going to be good. Sarah looked concerned in front of her and she felt she needed to do something to calm her down.

Offering a small smile she shrugged. "It's been happening," she said. "Sometimes I say some weird stuff, but I'm trying not to."

Sarah stared at her and tried to figure out what was going on. "What happens if you do?" she asked, watching her carefully and not touching her as she did.

"Then I don't get to go back to school," Alice said. "My f— Dad said I'm already on thin ice, so no doing anything that will make him mad so I can come back." She wouldn't look at Sarah as she said it, not wanting to see the look on her face or in her eyes as she did. It would just earn her pity and she didn't know what she was supposed to do with that.

There was a moment where nothing happened and Alice kept her eyes forward, looking down on the door and forcing her body to not fidget as she took in a few breaths. She didn't know what she was going to do until anything else happened, but then Sarah took her by the chin again and kept going with the eyeliner. "Here," she said, finishing up her eyes. "You let me talk tonight. You're coming to visit me this year for New Year's."

Alice took a deep, calming breath. "Thanks," she said. She felt a measure of relief, not sure why or what Sarah was going to do. So long as she behaved tonight it would be okay. Even if Sarah didn't do whatever it was she was trying to do, she wouldn't do anything that would ruin Alice's chances of not going back to school at the very least.

She hoped.

CHAPTER 4

California

ADRIANNA WAS ALMOST positive that Sarah was missing some of the story, but it didn't really matter. She did it. Not only did she find out how Alice was doing, but somehow got her father to let her come visit them. She didn't know how, but she had and Adrianna was willing to let her stay silent on the matter. All Sarah would say was that Alice was grounded and bored. Sarah had something else she wanted to say about it, but she became very careful with her words. That much, she could understand. There were a lot of things about Alice that she did not talk about.

Sarah had a large beach house and her mother let them stay in it with minimal parental supervision. Though Sarah warned that her mother might come around now and then, she was busy most of the day with work and events, so Rayne would be in charge. Rayne had come, as had Lance, who was there to make sure Adrianna didn't get in too much trouble.

They invited Adam with the intention that he would refuse given the long list of requirements Sarah had put on him should he show up. He declined, instead opting to spend the holidays with the rest of their family and taking Lance's place in Evan's wedding preparations that dominated the house now that Christmas had passed. He thought he'd prefer it to being nice to Alice.

It was the warmest winter that Adrianna had ever seen and she wasn't sure how to feel about it. It was still nice here, almost sunny most days, and she had no need for a winter coat. Adrianna had spent the morning watching the water lapping on the coast while drinking a hot chocolate that felt far too warm for the weather, even if Sarah thought it was chilly.

As everyone trickled in, Adrianna watched Sarah help Rob settle in. When Kevin appeared a few hours later, she let Rob take over as tour guide. Adrianna said nothing, though she caught the looks between the two of them and she would have to ask later if there was anything happening there. She didn't know what Kevin's deal was, but she didn't know how to ask and hoped she could figure out the words.

Gradually, they gathered in the large living room on the second floor overlooking the water. Rayne was out on the balcony, watching the waves with Adrianna. They said nothing, enjoying the sound and sight, so strange after so many New York winters. Kevin came out to join them.

"Hey," he said, looking out at the water. He didn't look like he was expecting to see anyone up there with Adrianna, but he recovered from his surprise and remembered how to introduce himself. He held out a hand and smiled cordially. "I'm Kevin," he said.

"Rayne," she said. "I'm Alice's sister."

"Ah, you're the missing Lori. Rayne?" he asked.

"Rayne," she said. "Only Alice gets to call me Lori anymore. I hope they haven't been telling you too much about me."

He laughed, embarrassed and not sure what to think. It was clear to Adrianna at least that he hadn't been expecting her to look like that, if nothing else. He kept trying so hard not to look at the hair. There was something else in his eyes as he watched her, a question on his lips, but he held it back for the moment.

"Only good things," Adrianna told him quickly. "No Heather?" she asked.

Kevin shook his head. "I tried talking to her, but she can't afford it. And you know her, she will not take a trip if you offer it."

"What about Peter?" Adrianna asked.

"Visiting a friend," he said. "John. They're starting to get along a little bit again. It's probably good for him. He's been having a lot of trouble being alone lately. I'm not sure if I should be worried."

"Little brother?" Rayne asked. She smiled as he nodded. "Younger siblings get a little clingy sometimes. Enjoy it while you can. Sometimes you have to abandon them for a couple years and they grow up without you and you can't do a lot to protect them at all. Just let them cling while they can."

"Oh, he's not a clingy kid," Kevin said. "He's just… There's some stuff going on. And he likes Alice. But, like, not that way. Something about her, he's just comfortable around her."

"Speaking of," Rayne said, tailing off as she noticed a set of headlights rolling into the driveway. She waited exactly long enough for a door to open before she made her way to the stairs. "If you'll excuse me, I'm going to help her get her stuff in."

"Bring her phone and computer in here first," Rob called after her, barely looking up.

Adrianna trailed after her, lingering at the door and waiting for her turn. Rayne was her family and she deserved to be the one to meet Alice at the car, scooping her up into a hug so hard it lifted Alice off the ground. Alice straightened herself out when Rayne put her down and paid the driver while Rayne went to get her suitcase. Alice looked like she was about to stop her, but Rayne was much too fast, grabbing Alice's hand in hers and dragging them both back to the house.

"Your turn," she said, passing Alice's hand to Adrianna's like a baton as she walked past. "I'll get this into your room."

Adrianna followed with a hug and brought Alice inside. "Hey," she said, trying to remember if Alice had always been that small. "How was the trip?"

"Fine."

"You look really tired."

Alice shrugged. "I'm okay. When did you get here?"

"A couple hours ago. Lance is here too. Adam didn't make it."

It wasn't until Alice's silence that she realized that she'd been expected to explain his absence. Sarah had been clear. She wasn't dealing with any bad energy when she was bringing in the new year, and that meant Adam was either going to have to play nice or not come. He had decided not coming was best, instead getting caught up in the whirlwind of wedding planning and going to fittings for both of them despite being a few sizes larger than Lance.

"You," Rob snapped at them when they came up the stairs. "Computer. Phone."

"You can say hi first," Kevin told him with a nudge.

"Hi," Rob said. "Computer. Phone. Now."

Obediently, Alice emptied out her backpack of her computer and phone, a book on African geography slipping out at the same time. Kevin snatched it up before Alice could grab it back, looking quizzically at it and then back to her. "Really?" he asked, flipping it open. His expression changed, eyes narrowing on the pages as he brought the book away from him. "Since when is Hogsmeade in Africa?"

Alice went very still and looked like she might run. It lasted only a moment, but Adrianna saw her go tense before her shoulders fell. "I didn't want to ruin the cover."

"Didn't you already finish this?" he passed the book back to her.

She grabbed it back, tucking it back in her bag. "I still like it," she said.

"*Lance get over here!*" Rob called into the house. "I am not going to be the only one dealing with this headache."

"What are you doing?" Rayne asked, coming in and leaning over the back of Rob's chair. "I'm not going to have to call someone, am I? I really don't want to have to *actually* chaperone while I'm here."

"Your dad put some crazy shit on her computer," he said. "I don't really know how to get this stuff off. I know Lance has some sort of hidden partition on here, but I've got no idea what he thought he was doing when he set this up."

He said the last part directly to Lance as he came in,

handing him Alice's computer. Lance took it, smirking as he dropped onto the couch and opened it to look through it. "I thought it should be difficult to find. Hidden and all that."

"Hey Alice," Sarah said, smiling at her before turning to the boys on the couch. "Now that we're all here, I'm thinking pizza? And when you guys are done with that, wanna head down to the beach? Someone started a bonfire."

"Are we going to have time for pizza and a bonfire?" Adrianna asked.

Sarah made a dismissive sound and waved the question away. "We're bringing the pizza to the fire. Best way to make friends. You in?"

Adrianna looked around, but she inevitably let her eyes rest on Rayne. She wasn't the only one, Rob glancing back and Kevin outright looking at her like he was expecting an answer.

Rayne let out a laugh at the attention. "What are you looking at me for?" she asked, laughing. "I'm not stopping you. I'm coming with you if you go and making sure you little hooligans get back here at the end of the night. Just don't make me have to chase you down."

ADRIANNA WASN'T SURE what to make of the

other people around the bonfire that night. There were a few families, mostly with kids their age and a little younger, and a few smaller children huddled around the large fire with marshmallows and blankets. They looked like they knew one another and regarded the teenagers with suspicion when they approached, their blue-haired chaperone not helping their first impression.

Sarah presented them all with pizza and they were quickly folded in from that alone. They were quickly talking to the others their own age about where they were from and what they were doing here, exchanging numbers and suggesting that they hang out during the break. Rayne fell in with the adults, making a few loud comments about the kids before offering to help distribute the food.

Even Alice looked like she was having fun. She'd ended up with Kevin talking to a guy on the other side of the fire and it looked like this new friend was hilarious. Knowing she was okay, Adrianna let herself calm down, paying more attention to the boy who had joined her and Sarah.

"It's actually our house," the boy named Aiden told them. "We come out here every New Year's. It's usually dead. It's not really beach weather in December, you know?"

"It's not bad," Sarah told him. "You just have to try a little harder."

He laughed at that. "You guys should join us on New

Year's," he said, smiling at Adrianna. "The parents are heading into town, so it's just going to be a few of us. You're all more than welcome."

Sarah handed him her phone. "Give me your number," she said. "We'll let you know."

Aiden gladly took it and put his number in. When he handed it back, he looked like he might have been redder, though it was hard to tell in the orange light of the fire. They stood quietly for a moment before he looked back to his parents and excused himself.

Sarah smiled as she went back to her phone and Adrianna slipped in next to her, smiling and speaking quietly. "I thought you and Wyatt..."

"Oh, I'm not calling him," Sarah said, the grin not leaving her face and her eyes going back to him. "It's just better he give me his than I give him mine. He seems like he could be really fun, though."

Adrianna had to agree, though she caught Lance giving him a glare in moments between a chat he was having with another girl. Even as she looked after him, her eyes trailed back to Rayne and to Alice who was next to her, saying something quietly. Their conversation was short, Rayne nodding and Alice wandering away from the fire.

She watched as Alice walked away from them and back toward the house, her mind wandering in circles. Wasn't she having fun? It looked like everyone else had been. She had been laughing. Should Adrianna have been paying more attention, have made sure she was okay? Should she go after her and make sure she was okay now?

A hand on her shoulder stopped her and she looked back to see Rayne watching her sister head back to the house. "This is a lot for her," she said gently. "Just give her a bit. She'll be okay."

Adrianna watched as Alice walked alone back down the beach to the house. Letting out a sigh, she nodded and let Rayne lead her back to the bonfire. If Rayne wasn't worried, she shouldn't be either. And, as Aiden came closer with an extra skewer with a marshmallow for her, she decided that it would be fine to stay a little longer.

CHAPTER 5

Cracks

IF SHE WAS being honest, Alice wasn't that interested in reading *Harry Potter and the Order of the Phoenix* again. She had read the series again and again because it had been there and she read it now because it was the easiest way to pass the time until everyone else got back. Her phone and computer were sitting in the living room, but she wasn't sure if they were really done with them yet, so she couldn't try picking up Robert's Clockpunk game to see if it was more stimulating.

Not that she wanted stimulating. She had been around new people, made small talk, but after a day of travel she just wanted to rest. They had been nice, but one of the boys kept getting a bit too close and Alice didn't want to keep hiding behind Kevin all night. After all, he was having fun. She was just tired from the trip. Lori was fine with her heading back early, and that was all the permission she needed to allow herself to have that quiet.

Still, she wished she had a different book. She was reading it now and was already bored with it. Still, she went through, line by line and page by page, trying very hard to get lost in it. It was almost meditative, reading more for the sake of reading than to actually enjoy the escape.

"Alice? Are you okay?"

Alice didn't look up from the book as Adrianna let herself into their room. "Yeah," Alice said. "Just tired."

"Do you want to talk about it?"

Alice finished the page and pinched it, closing the book on her fingers. Like it knew what was going on, her head started to throb and tug at the edges, Alice knowing that if she wasn't careful she might let something strange out of her mouth. But Adrianna knew that she would do something like that. And, from how she was looking at her, Alice knew that brand of concern was about Wonderland.

"I'm not done over there yet," Alice said. She tried to keep her words perfectly sane to keep her from worrying, knowing that the content of them would do enough of that anyway. "But I can't get back over to finish anything. The Mad Hatter gave me his hat like it was supposed to help, but I can't even take it out."

"You could take it out now," Adrianna said, getting up.

"You don't have to tell Rayne what it is. She probably won't even ask. She's just happy you're here. Where did you put it?"

Alice hadn't even thought of what Lori might think. Her sister was sharing the room with her instead of Adrianna, which meant she would have to be a lot more careful about the contents of her suitcase. She wondered if there was a gap in the roof or the floorboards to hide the books hidden under her clothes.

She was so tired. Shaking her head, she opened the book again and went back to it. Adrianna didn't even like Wonderland. She didn't know why she was so interested in ways for her to get back now. "It's in my suitcase," Alice said. "I'm not supposed to go back anyway. I have to stay here now."

"You still have to put the hearts back, right?" Adrianna said. She opened Alice's suitcase and started rifling through it. "Once you finish that, then you're done, though. And you'll be back here. But that's not so bad, right? You'll find something to do here. You have friends here. It's not so bad out here. And you know Wonderland was going to send you back here again eventually, right?"

Alice did nothing to stop her, letting her mind drift again over the book. Even this made her miss Wonderland. Harry got to go back to his terrible, magical world every year. Alice wished it were that easy for her, if it were so simple as just leaving one day and heading back to it without anyone or anything that would stop her. That someone might actually want her there enough that they would come get her.

And for just a moment, she was there again. Instead of the soft, lapping waves of the ocean outside the window, she was staring out at the window of the White Rabbit's house. There was the garden outside and, though she could still hear the ocean, she wanted so badly to hear what was happening in Wonderland instead. To know if they had gotten the hearts. If things were just the way she remembered it.

She knew they wouldn't be, though. She had left Morgana there in the Queen of Heart's place. Morgana wanted to do something about the two worlds, to take over Wonderland and Neverland for some purpose that was lost on Alice. She seemed perfectly content to leave the castle lodged directly into the wall that kept the worlds apart for some reason. There was something about it that made Alice certain that nothing would be just as she wanted to remember it. It had surely changed, and so her daydream was only that.

"She's almost got it," something said quietly, too quietly for her to really tell if she was hearing it at all.

"That's not possible," she heard much more clearly. "She probably just slipped out while you weren't looking. You know how she is."

Alice let out a sigh, accepting that she was by the ocean and there were people who were going to be asking for her company again soon enough. Adrianna wouldn't have returned alone, after all. She could hear the rumblings behind her, of people talking in the hall and of a movie playing downstairs. She should go and join them.

But still, she stayed sitting at the window, trying to read a book she was bored with. She didn't want to get into the conversation happening out in the hall. She was only partially listening, not wanting to accept that the conversation was about her.

She could just appear downstairs, but there was no way for her to know who was where in this house and who was paying attention to her. There were too many people and they were not following patterns she was familiar with. They would know if she was doing anything unusual. She just wanted to slip into the back of a room and be there without interacting, participating just enough so they wouldn't talk about her.

She wondered if this house had cameras too. If they could see her right now. The page creased under her fingers and she let it go.

Of course there weren't. Sarah wouldn't have cameras in her house.

The door opened again and Alice let out a sigh, turning back around and seeing Adrianna and Lance standing in the doorway. Adrianna was pale at seeing her, breathless and eyes wide. "Where did you go?" Adrianna asked. "You… you disappeared."

Alice looked at her, trying to figure out what she was talking about. "I've just been here," Alice said. "I'll come down, though." She got to her feet, coming to join them. "What are they watching down there? It sounds like a weird movie."

"You were gone," Adrianna said. "You just…"

"Maybe head downstairs," Lance said gently. "We'll catch up."

Adrianna looked like she was about to argue before she went very quiet. She looked back at Alice, staring at her for a moment, but she said nothing and went upstairs without them. Lance watched her go before she went into the room, his eyes going first to the mirror before Alice. The smell of fire and sugar surrounded them and she wondered if Adrianna had also smelled like this and she hadn't noticed. She closed the book again, still pinching her page, and waited.

"Is there anything you need to say?"

"Sorry," Alice said, not quite looking at him and looking back toward where Adrianna had been standing. Maybe she would have been less upset if Alice had been paying proper attention instead of trying to read a book she didn't care about. She should really just put it down. "I wasn't listening before. I think I made her mad. I didn't think she could get mad."

Lance stopped, narrowing his eyes on her. "She said you disappeared."

Alice wished, but that wasn't going to happen. "I can't really do that right now," she said, her voice going very quiet. "I mean, I can, but someone's going to see."

"She said she was talking to you and you vanished. She thought you went out the window or something."

Alice blinked. "I don't have to go out the window, though. I can just... You know. But I don't want Lori or someone else to see. I don't know how to explain it. And if my dad found out—"

"Okay," Lance told her quickly. "Okay."

Alice realized she was starting to panic amidst the pounding in her head and Lance was trying to stop her. Her heart was already racing, terrified of what her father knowing might mean. She didn't know what else she might have to do if he found out that she could disappear and reappear wherever she wanted. He already didn't want her leaving the house and watched her every move. If he knew she could just vanish, then she didn't know what he would do to her for breaking his rules.

"Sorry," Alice said.

Lance looked tired from dealing with her already. "Don't," he told her. "Just don't."

"You're going to have to be much more precise than

don't," Alice told him crossly, her embarrassment turned to agitation in an instant. "There are a great many things that could be done, and I am never going to be able to follow through with which if you do not specify. Don't stand, don't breathe, don't speak perhaps?"

"What?" Lance stepped back at the sudden shift. "Alice, are you—"

"Though if I may offer a don't, perhaps don't be so demanding when I am trying so very hard to be accommodating. A thank you for what efforts I am affording would go over much better than an insistence to cease a thing you do not specify."

But his eyes weren't on her any longer, instead trailing behind her. "Alice, what happened there?"

Alice looked back, following his eyes. Behind her in the mirror in the room, she could see mostly a reflection of the room. In it, though, there was a crack in the mirror showing something else. Wonderland was staring back at her, changed and dark, but definitely Wonderland in a very thin line behind the glass.

Alice's eyes went wide and she ran back to it, staring at it for a moment before she reached a hand up to touch it. Lance was faster, grabbing her hand and keeping her fingers from making contact with the glass. From going back. She gasped and tugged before she looked back at him. She was shaking, she could tell now that she saw her wavering wrist in his steady hand. She could feel herself starting to cry, but tried to push it down.

"You can't go right now," Lance told her, his voice low and eyes darting back to the open door. "Not here. Someone's going to notice."

She looked back at it. It was only a crack of Wonderland looking back at her, but it was there. She pulled her hand back and backed away from the mirror and him, not sure what to do. She wanted to run and jump into it, but she knew the crack wasn't nearly enough for her to get through. And Lance was in her way. Lance wasn't going to let her get through.

"What's going on, Alice?"

"It's been gone," Alice told him, her voice shaking. She was shaking, relief and fear washing over her. She couldn't get in through just those cracks. They were too small. But she could see it again, and that was maybe enough. It would have to be enough. "They wouldn't let me come back. I couldn't even see. What's happening over there? It's dark. It's never dark in Wonderland."

"You can't go back right now."

Alice took a deep, steadying breath. She wiped the tears from her eyes and tried to force herself to calm down. "I can't," she said. "The cracks are too small. I can't get through."

Lance hesitated to say something else, but he took a deep

breath and nodded instead. "We should get back downstairs. Your sister is going to think we're up to something up here."

Alice nodded, staring at the cracks. Slowly, she closed her eyes and took another steadying breath. She could see Wonderland again. For right now that would be enough. Maybe she would hear Cat again, berating her for letting herself get into this situation. Or a voice yelling at her for being rude again. Something about that was enough to make her feel better.

When she opened her eyes, the cracks into Wonderland were gone from the mirror. She was still shaking, but she let Lance lead the way downstairs and far away from the mirror.

She tried to pull herself together, at least enough to be around friends who had no idea what Wonderland was. She needed to be around the people who would miss her so they wouldn't think that something had happened. There were people who would miss her now if she left. She found herself still looking in the corners of the halls, looking for something that might be watching her even now. But there was nothing here but the voices upstairs, all too distracted by a movie to notice her as she joined them on the couches.

She could see Wonderland again. And maybe those cracks would start getting bigger again. When they did, she could get back across and see for herself what was going on.

CHAPTER 6

The Deal

THE WEEK PASSED by too fast. Adrianna was a little sad they never met up with Aiden again but, true to her word, Sarah never called him and deleted his number as soon as they got back to the house. Between trips into town and hanging out on a beach that Sarah insisted was much too cold, they found plenty to do to occupy themselves. There had been fireworks a little further down from them and they had built chairs in the sand to sit and enjoy them at midnight when the new year rolled in.

Rayne agreed that Alice was having fun after a couple days. She spent a distressing amount of time staring at mirrors, but Adrianna was almost used to that now. She didn't disappear, though she caught her more than a few times reaching into an empty bag to pull out something she left behind. Once they found a bookstore for her to wander through, Alice was perfectly content. She even kept from burying herself in the new books immediately.

Of everyone, Lance attempted to make sure she was around and involved in everything they were doing. She got the distinct feeling he was keeping an eye on her, which made sense. He liked her. More than a few times, she wondered when he would finally ask her out, but Alice never said anything about it to her. She had no idea if she would say yes, but she couldn't think of a reason she wouldn't.

It was almost a shame to go back to school. The beach house had been so much fun and warm, and now they had to put coats back on for the light layer of snow. It wasn't even as nice as New York, where the snow really committed to flooding its way into your life. The snow at Lucena Academy always looked like it could wash away at any moment, which meant that she would just have to try to enjoy it as much as she could while it lasted. At least it made the place look and feel more magical, and she could use that feeling as classes started.

Alice left early that morning to the first Combat Club meeting of the new year, letting Adrianna stay in bed a little longer. She wasn't in there for long, waiting just long enough to know that Alice wouldn't be coming back for anything before she hopped out and locked the door. It wouldn't stop Alice from coming back in, but she would at least have some warning.

It was the first big secret she had ever kept from Alice and the first thing she had ever done that she felt guilty about. But only a little. It was really for the best.

She hid the white book under her mattress. Alice kept the rest of the books hidden away somewhere in the room, somewhere she could get to by making her hand disappear into thin air, but Adrianna had found this one on her own. Inside the Mad Hatter's hat in Alice's suitcase under a bottom that was marked *Pull me*, was a book that had a cover that attracted a breeze. She had reached into the hat and pulled out the book, only to look up and find Alice gone. And when Alice came back, she didn't mention the book, keeping it for herself.

Alice had already promised to let Adrianna work with the books now, given that she was better with them and could actually pronounce the words on the pages, though Adrianna was sure that she had to work harder to make anything in them work. Something about watching Alice do things, it seemed like once she learned something she just knew it. Adrianna had to work so hard every time with these spells to make them work properly.

This book was about traveling and moving from one place to another as near as she could figure. There were bits in here about teleporting, and there were other things about moving between things that were much more conceptual. It was about moving parts of yourself or all of yourself to other places, whether those places were real or not. About what to do if you tried to go somewhere that didn't exist and got stuck there.

But she couldn't spend all morning trying to make sense of it. After an hour, she put it back under her mattress and hopped into the shower. At least if Alice disappeared again this book looked like it would give Adrianna a way to figure out how to find her again. Alice lied often enough to try to save herself, almost as if she didn't realize she was doing it, and Adrianna suspected that her disappearing at the beach house wasn't just an accident. She had stopped, but Adrianna knew it was only a matter of time before she did it again.

Adrianna got herself ready and went down to get a late breakfast with the others. Looking around the cafeteria, she spotted Rob and Kevin sitting with Sarah at one of the tables. She waved at Adrianna as she came over to join them.

"Hey," Kevin said as she came over with her food. "Arthur's looking for you. Thought you should know."

Adrianna sat up a little straighter and frowned as she watched him. "Why?"

Kevin shrugged. "He was asking about you yesterday. Said you owed him something."

"Oh," Adrianna said, poking at her pancakes. Her appetite abandoned her. "I forgot about that."

"Tell me it's, like, five bucks or something," Sarah said, watching her. "He seems like a dick."

"He's not that bad," Adrianna said. As much as she dreaded encountering him again, she couldn't blame him entirely for what was going on. He was in a strange new world he didn't want to be in and he was trying to adjust. That he did that by holding her brother hostage and following her around, she didn't like, but still she felt some sympathy for him. "I mean, he is, but he's just—"

"You have a problem, Addie," Sarah told her. "You can't help everyone. And you have your hands full trying to fix Alice, you don't need another project."

"Aren't you trying to fix Alice too?" Robert asked, looking sidelong at Sarah.

"I just needed to get her out of that house because that was scary," Sarah said. "She's all Addie's now."

"Are you finally going to tell us what happened in there?"

"Not talking about it," Sarah told him quickly. "We are done, it's over, never again. Alice one hundred percent makes sense now and I wish I could unlearn all of that. Now, what happened with Arthur? What do you owe him?"

"A date?"

Sarah stared at her dumbfounded for a moment, mouth open and gaping at her. Suddenly, she shut her mouth and looked away. "I'm done with both of you. Room 201 is dead to me."

Kevin was staring at her, dumbfounded and shaking his head. "*How?*"

"It's not that bad," Adrianna said. "He did a favor and said I could pay him back with a date. It's just one date. Maybe he won't be that bad if I get to know him a little more." Maybe she could convince him to let Lance go.

"He's hot," Sarah said. "But he's also that bad."

"Say it a little louder," Robert told her, nudging her and nodding across the room.

Arthur had just come in with Lance, heading for the line to get food. Adrianna could see that Lance wasn't here right now. He hadn't been since they got back to school. At least he wasn't dead, but Adrianna missed her brother and hated that he was being held over her head. He looked so happy over there, laughing and smiling, but he didn't even look the same to her anymore.

Over the summer, he had said the ghost was nice and didn't want to be there either. That they were working together in a way, and it wasn't enough to get pulled out of school over to avoid. Maybe if she gave Arthur the chance, he would let the ghost out and let her have her brother back.

Still, Adrianna turned back hoping Arthur wouldn't see her. The rest of them humored her, letting her think she would be safe, but she knew full well from their eyes watching that Arthur had spotted her and was on his way. Not that she needed their eyes with how loud Arthur and Lance were as they made their approach.

"Hey, miss me?" Arthur said, leaning around Adrianna's chair and putting his tray down next to her. "Hey," he said to the rest of the table, Lance taking a seat on his other side and settling on the table. "Good Christmas? I heard you guys were off on the beach for New Year's. That must have been fun for you."

He didn't need to specify that he was irritated about not being invited. It was obvious in the way he had said it, and from the way he looked between Rob and Kevin until his gaze fell silently on Sarah. She looked back at him, no smile on her face and no attempt to be polite or accommodating. Instead, it almost looked like she was daring him to say something about it, but she didn't say a word.

Adrianna smiled cordially, looking over at her brother to make sure he was still okay. He looked fine, at least, though it wasn't him at all. He smiled too wide, sat too straight, and looked far too relaxed in his seat. She never noticed how Lance held himself until he wasn't himself anymore. Now it was too much like Matt when he had won something.

She wondered if that white book would have a way to bring Matt back. But this wasn't the time to get distracted.

"It was good," Adrianna said when no one else took the conversational bait. She knew what she owed Arthur and it would do no good to pretend that it wouldn't happen. Not while he was flaunting control of her brother. Maybe it wouldn't be so bad, and maybe she could find something good in him. "I'm sure Lance already told you all about it."

"Oh, he did," he said, glaring back at him. There was a look that crossed Lance's face, one of fatigue and just a little pain that resettled into the smile from before. The way Arthur looked at him, it was clear that was intentional, but Lance didn't let it show for long. Arthur looked back at her casually and nodded. "So, what are you doing tomorrow? I thought we could hang out."

"I have choir at three," she told him. Sunday choir practice would at least keep the date short.

"I promise it will be more fun with me."

"She said she has practice," Kevin chimed in, irritated. When Arthur looked at him, Kevin raised an eyebrow in question. "If you wanted to pressure her into saying yes, maybe you don't do it in front of her friends."

"I think she can decide for herself," Arthur said, turning his attention back to her.

Across the table, Lance flinched and that look of pain crossed his face. He squashed it quickly, but not before Adrianna had caught it. Worse, she could still see the pain in his eyes as he tried to hide it. She could hardly believe he was being so brazen, that he would use her brother to make her say yes in front of her friends. They could do this another time, without all the people, but it had to be here and now.

Adrianna had never hated anyone so much before, and her attempts to try to look at this positively were falling flat. No matter how she wanted to remind herself that Arthur was alone here, in a world he was unfamiliar with and probably scared, he was still hurting people. Her family. Her sympathy was wearing thin and, though she clung to it, she couldn't bring herself to fully commit to trying to find the good in him if he would keep doing things like this to her.

"I'll skip choir tomorrow," Adrianna told him. Her friends looked upset about it, but they all stayed quiet and let her make the choice. It was clear no one liked this decision, but at least they wouldn't try to stop her. Not while Arthur was still here, at least.

Lance shook his head and frowned as he glared back at Arthur. Though Arthur didn't give a second thought to what he was doing, Lancelot's ghost at least looked offended that it had happened and, though Arthur wasn't paying any attention to him as he basked in his victory, Adrianna could tell Lancelot was not happy with him.

The moment passed quickly and the grin was back. He looked behind Arthur, his head nodding upward and he gave a small wave to someone behind them. "How do you guys feel about a little company?" he asked. "Hey Alice, you busy tomorrow?"

Adrianna looked back, seeing Alice and Heather coming to join them. Alice looked surprised to have any attention paid to her, but Heather gave her a small bump of her hip, grinning and quietly encouraging her. It was good to see Heather and Alice getting along, at least. "No?" she asked, looking around the table and trying to figure out what she was getting herself into. She didn't shrink at the question, though she moved more slowly next to Heather. "Why?"

"Double date. You in?" The smile didn't leave his face as he asked, like he was expecting a yes and had no shame. Which he didn't anymore.

It was so brazen that Adrianna was shocked he would say it. Then again, that wasn't Lance in there right now. And if she didn't have to be alone with Arthur, she would take Alice's backup. She could help her get out of there if something happened. She would understand better than anyone else what was really happening.

That Arthur wasn't protesting was a surprise to her, though she had a guess why he might be okay with having them there. Hurting her brother was a very easy way to get Adrianna to be compliant, and if he didn't have that leverage over her, she was planning to keep it as short as possible.

Her mind was already turning as she looked back at Alice. "Please?" she asked.

She could see Alice thinking, looking from Lance to Adrianna and back again, confusion soon turning into compliance. "Sure," she said after a moment. Adrianna knew it was probably because there were just too many people watching her, and Heather goading her on was not helping her think clearly. She smiled back at Lance. "I suppose the plans to sit around and stare at walls will just have to wait for another day."

Sarah, on the other hand, looked entirely disappointed in them. Adrianna felt her phone vibrate in her pocket and she pulled it out, turning on the screen to find a message from Sarah waiting at her. She glanced across the table, but Sarah was no longer paying attention to them.

Sarah

Later.

It was the period that let her know how much Sarah disapproved of what was happening, but it was too late now. Adrianna nodded and they settled into breakfast, talking and chatting like nothing was wrong at all. Arthur took his leave now that he had what he wanted, taking Lance with him, and Adrianna promised Alice she would explain later. Alice went along with it and let everyone else talk about how much they didn't like Arthur or what he could have done to make Adrianna owe him a date.

But it was a perfect plan. Lance liked Alice and Alice needed something else to think about other than Wonderland. Whatever he had said to her back at the beach house had been enough to keep her from disappearing again and keep her where she was. He somehow calmed her down and she was more social than Adrianna had ever seen her. Lance was good for her and if there was anyone who could help her figure out how to get Lance free of the spirit that Arthur had forced into him, it was Alice. They could come up with some kind of plan for it and maybe Alice could help her figure out how to do it before tomorrow. If they could get away to do that kind of research today.

At least it looked like Heather and Alice were getting along. That was a nice change. And Heather looked surprisingly calm, though her expression went sour at Kevin. "Is there something going on with your brother?" she asked. "He's been off at club."

"He's not sleeping well," Kevin said, shrugging. "No big deal."

Adrianna caught Alice's eye and silently asked if she knew what was going on. Alice thought about it for a moment before she mouthed back, *Neverland*. Her face said she wasn't sure about it.

Adrianna frowned, but said nothing more about it. Kevin looked like he was already dealing with it and she had tomorrow to worry about. Besides, Neverland was not the thing that was affecting her family right now. For right now, Neverland could be a Kevin problem and she could focus her attention on Wonderland and what she would do about tomorrow.

CHAPTER 7

Escapsim

HER HEAD WAS pounding, so Alice tried not to talk. Her friends had tolerated the strangeness during the break, but now that they were back in school, dressed in their uniforms and surrounded by teachers, she knew better than to let too much slip out. Even when she did say something odd, they barely seemed to notice, though Alice had to wonder if that was only them being polite. Either way, she was much more careful on school grounds.

The library was a relief. She had a shift there and slipped away to retreat into the stacks. Kevin was there as well, but he didn't follow her, taking his stack in a different direction and letting Alice have her space.

She was grateful for it, letting out a breath and closing her eyes as she leaned against one of the shelves. She could feel the throbbing even in her eyes and it was only getting worse. When her eyes opened again, she looked around and she started putting away the books slowly, wandering to an area that looked unoccupied.

"Better to know or not to know?" Alice asked herself very quietly. Her head was pounding so badly that she needed to do something to relieve it and she couldn't see anyone around to hear her this far in the back corner. "Ignorance is bliss and bliss is a very lovely state to be in. But being blissful for too long means you may never truly appreciate the bliss for you will never know anything else."

Another book went back on the shelf as she made her way to the bright colors of the back corner of the library. People were either very proud to venture back there or scared to be caught amidst the rainbows. Today it was barren and she was mercifully alone.

"Not that I've ever known bliss," she reminded herself. "Perhaps a taste of bliss would do me some good. After all, no one wants to be around someone who looks miserable all the time. A smile is a lie, and a lie hides only so much. Unless it is a very good lie."

Alice's eyes strayed to her reflection in the window and the other things there. She couldn't always see the cracks, but she always knew when they were there and today they were following her. They almost felt like they were watching her, like they knew she was ready to run over as soon as one was large enough. Not that she should. She had something to do tomorrow. Adrianna and Lance both wanted her to go on a date.

She looked around at the books in this part of the library. Their collection of gender and sexuality books was still small, with lots of open space on the shelves as if they were planning to one day fill them. She looked over the titles, remembering the emails Lori had sent her last semester. She asked her to stop after that one about asexuality, saying she was too busy with school to keep up. Looking at the books now, she couldn't see any of the stripes of purple or green or gray that she had seen in that email on the spines.

No, it probably wasn't actually a thing. She just hadn't found the right person yet.

At least she knew she wasn't gay. Lori told her what it was like and Alice could confirm that she had never felt that way when she was around pretty girls, so she was safe in that regard at least. Lori had already gotten kicked out over that and she had been the favorite of the two of them. If Alice was interested in girls, she didn't know what her father would do.

And she had a good chance of falling for Lance. He was attractive, and that was all most people seemed to need to fall for someone. She'd known him for a while and she did like hanging out with him. She was sure she could fall for him if she tried hard enough. After all, if Adrianna could like

Arthur enough to go out with him, then Alice could make herself like Lance with enough effort.

"It's not polite to stare," Alice said. She could feel the cracks watching her. "If you must, at least invite me in. I would much prefer to be there. My thoughts are becoming much too loud and Wonderland is much quieter. Not nice of you to keep all that quiet to yourself."

At least her headache was starting to fade. Sometimes Alice wondered if it was the talking that helped or if it was just seeing Wonderland there on the other side of the reflection. It was darker now, but the colors were still there. Sometimes she could see flowers or a flash of green, or something moving on the other side. It always seemed to show the same place, though, which was odd. And there was never any purple, which was odder.

Wonderland's cracks faded away again and she was left alone in the library, holding a stack of books that were not meant for this section. Looking at the books now, she felt more isolated than alone and she shifted her stack of books in her arms. She should get back to putting these back.

She wandered back into the sciences sections of the stacks and started to put the books back until her arms were empty again. Still, her mind wanted to wander, so she went back to get more books. Maybe fiction this time, something that she could read while she was putting them away so she didn't have to think too much about anything.

None of the novels looked that interesting, but when her mind started to wander, she opened up the first book in the stack and started to read. Alice didn't know when she developed the skills required to read and walk and do work at the same time, but reading didn't slow her down from getting the books into their proper spots.

Kevin appeared next to her, bending down to put something back before leaning over her shoulder to see what she was looking at. "What's it about?" he asked.

"I don't know yet."

"I think they made it into a movie."

Alice frowned, looking at the cover. She hadn't really paid attention to what it was. Flipping to the cover, she saw it was *The Handmaid's Tale* and tried to remember if she'd heard anything else about it. "Isn't this something we have to read next year?" she asked.

"I think it depends who you get." Kevin lingered, shifting the books in his arms. "So. Addie and Arthur."

"Yeah, I guess."

"Do you know what he's got on her?" he asked. "She said she owed him for something."

"She never told me about it." Alice shrugged. She wasn't

sure what to make of the look on Kevin's face, of the disbelief and the concern. "Maybe she just likes him."

"Why?"

"He's hot?" She wasn't sure what he wanted from her. Sometimes people went out with people because they were attractive and then realized they were nice enough to properly fall in love with them. She had enough examples of that in the stack of books in her hands. "I don't know."

"Something is weird about it," Kevin said. "At least you and Lance are going to be there."

Alice nodded. She didn't really want to think about that part of it. "What about you and Robert? You could come too."

Kevin stopped, staring at her. He went pale at the question. His mouth opened and then sealed itself shut again. Alice played with the corner of the pages of the books, waiting until he found his words again. "Have you talked to Peter?" he asked.

Alice frowned. Thoughts started stirring in the back of her mind, but she didn't know which thing she should be worried about. "No. Why?"

"You said he gave up Neverland, right?" he asked quietly. "That's all done?"

"Did something happen?" she asked. He looked worried about something.

"He's having trouble sleeping still. And he keeps waking up in weird places. He..." Kevin paused, looking around as he struggled to find the words.

"Flies?" Alice offered.

Kevin looked surprised, but he put the books in his hands down on the shelves next to them. One by one, he started organizing them, not looking at Alice as he spoke. "He's waking up all over campus. He doesn't know how he gets there, but he thinks he's waking up farther and farther away. He doesn't know what's going on."

"Peter's never been that observant," Alice said dismissively. "And it seems he's not very good at sleeping if his body doesn't understand what's happening. Perhaps his body just needs a good stern talking to so it understands that night is a time for stillness and not more play. Though perhaps he has been too preoccupied with work and his body has seen no other way but to seize any chance at play that—"

Alice forced her mouth shut, catching her words a little too late. She was ready to apologize, to tell him that she meant none of it. To just forget everything.

But Kevin wasn't watching her anymore. His eyes were on the window. Alice turned back, seeing a crack to Wonderland in the mirror and a pair of familiar brown eyes staring back at her. Eyes like the ones she saw every day watching from across her dorm room. A moment later, they closed and faded away, leaving only the view of the school grounds.

CHAPTER 8

Attempted Plans

ADRIANNA FINALLY GOT Alice alone after she got back from the library. She returned with a new pile of books to drown herself in during her spare moments. She had gone from looking at the magic books in her every spare moments to novels and Adrianna wasn't sure which was better in the long run. For now, neither. They had work to do.

"We need a plan for tomorrow," Adrianna said as Alice dropped her books on her desk.

"What's tomorrow?"

"The date!"

"Oh," Alice said. "Right. Why did you say yes to Arthur? Kevin thinks there's something going on."

"He wouldn't break that curse on you otherwise," Adrianna said.

Just when Adrianna's guilt came back and she thought

she should apologize, Alice shrugged and sat on her bed. "I forgot about that," Alice mumbled, her head dipping into her hand for just a moment before she looked back up. "So what do we need a plan for? A date is only a date, and you've done that before. Unless this date is not meant to be a date, which seems most unseemly."

"It's still going to be a date," Adrianna insisted, seeing something flicker at the edge of her vision. "But we're going to do something else as well. We need to come up with a plan."

"What's wrong?" Alice asked.

The thing flickering out of the corner of her eye stopped when Adrianna glanced again, seeing only a mirror before she looked back to Alice. "Arthur's doing something to Lance still," she said. "I think he's going to keep using Lance for as long as he can keep that ghost in him. And we're going to try and figure out how to get that ghost out of there. If you think you can help me figure it out?"

Alice looked almost relieved and nodded. "Terribly rude to take another person for a ride without asking them first. I imagine Lance would have much rather preferred that he was asked first."

Adrianna smiled and Alice reached up, her arm disappearing for a moment to her elbow before she drew it back down, now with a stack of books balanced in her palm. "You want to use these, right?" she asked. "Arthur's magic is from these, so the way to get a ghost out should also be in here somewhere."

"Thanks," Adrianna said, taking the top book off of the pile. Again out of the corner of her eye, she could see something that she was pretty sure was not supposed to be there. This time, she looked at the mirror and she caught what it was she was seeing. What was sneaking into the corner of her vision constantly since the beach house.

A crack in the mirror. And another world peering out from the other side of it. Stranger, the cracks in it were getting larger.

Adrianna said nothing and flipped through the red book, feeling a chill run through her at the feeling of the cover under her hands. It felt like someone's skin and it was distracting enough that she didn't pay attention to the things on the other side of the mirror anymore. It was unsettling in a way that drew her attention away. But Wonderland was gone when she looked back.

"You said you couldn't go back, right?" Adrianna asked, still watching the mirror. She felt like something had been staring through those cracks int he mirror and she was not looking forward to Cat coming back through for a chat. "To Wonderland, I mean."

Alice looked up at her, then to the mirror. "Was it doing

it again?" she asked. "I'm sorry, it's been following me around a lot lately. Kevin looked pretty freaked out about it earlier, but he never said anything about it."

"You're not doing it?"

"I don't think so," Alice said. "It's just been watching. About as subtle as Arthur watching you. And possibly less wanted."

Adrianna looked at Alice as she shot a glare at the mirror, but she was soon looking down at the brown book in her lap again. She pored over the pages like they were homework, as if she weren't already intimately familiar with every inch of those books.

Adrianna quickly decided that the image of Alice reading novels was much better. She almost felt bad about dragging her into this, no matter how she might feel responsible for it. It was only a matter of time before Wonderland stopped calling her all together. At least she was learning how to live her life without it. Soon, they could all be free of it. There were just a couple things that needed to happen first.

She barely got back into the red book before her phone vibrated in her pocket. Sarah requested her presence at Bean and Adrianna excused herself to meet her. Alice didn't even look up from her side of the room, waving her away and continuing to read through the pages in search of anything that might help her deal with a ghost. It seemed like a strange thing to find in a book about beasts, but Adrianna didn't think about it until she was already out of the dorms.

She spotted Sarah sitting with Wyatt, who took his leave as soon as he spotted Adrianna. He smiled at her and nodded as he left, leaving his spot free for Adrianna to fill. Sarah watched her, waiting until she was at the small table before she said anything.

"This will be the only time I interfere," Sarah told her as she sat down, "so listen now. After this, you won't have me getting in the middle of anything else you guys have going on, you got it?"

"What's this about?"

"Are you really trying to get Alice to hook up with your brother?" she asked. "Alice. *Alice.*"

"It's not like—"

"And not even Lance," Sarah continued. "Whatever Lance becomes when he's around Arthur. And don't think no one's noticed. He was completely different over the break. There's some bullshit happening here. But you're really going to try to get your best friend and your brother to get together with how he is right now? With how she is in general?"

"It's not like that," Adrianna said, flustered and blushing. "I mean, not really. It's just…"

"So what's it like?" she asked, picking up her drink. "I'm listening. You have until I finish this."

"Sarah."

But she was already drinking, eyebrows raised. It was Adrianna's turn to come up with an explanation.

Adrianna looked at Sarah frowning before she looked around and made sure there was no one really listening to the two of them. "Arthur's done something to Lance and Alice is going to help me, you know, stop him from that. That's all. Alice is the only one who can help. You know she is."

Sarah nodded and put her drink down. Adrianna looked and saw she still had half of it left to go. Sarah had more that she wanted to say and she took a moment to collect her thoughts before she began. "And Lance having a crush on her is a total coincidence," she said. "Or hasn't he made that obvious enough yet?"

"I mean, if they end up liking each other that's not so—"

"Addie." Sarah looked tired. "Look. I love you. But you can't try to hook Alice up with someone right now. I don't care how nice your brother is when Arthur isn't around, you didn't see where she lives. Even if you think she's fine now, it's just because she's a lot safer here. That doesn't mean she's okay. Alice has that look in her eyes like she's in an abusive relationship. And you want her going out with Lance, who is an asshole right now."

Adrianna's resolve flickered and she felt a pang of guilt from dragging her into this, but this was the only way to get her brother back. It felt like an exaggeration designed to make her feel guilty about it. Sarah couldn't possibly know what was going on from visiting Alice's house twice. "She says it's fine."

"She probably thinks that," Sarah said, letting out a sigh. She reached across the table and took Adrianna by the wrist. "Look, maybe Lance will be good for her if he can be normal again. But I don't think it's a good idea now. Think back to the beach and New Year's. We were around a lot of people. Nice, attractive people. And did Alice look at even one of them?"

"I don't—"

"She didn't. And if she's not ready to start checking people out, she's not ready to start a relationship." Sarah drank the rest of her latte. "And that's all I have to say. It's all on you now. I'm not doing this anymore. I'm pulling a Heather and getting out of all of this, whatever it is."

Adrianna looked at her latte and nodded. "Thanks," she said, smiling back at Sarah as she got up.

Sarah gestured for Adrianna to get up and walk with her, heading back to the dorms. "Still love you both, but 201 is exhausting to deal with," she said. "I know you're dealing with a lot, but I got myself some counseling. And the school psych thinks I need to stop trying to get involved in things that I can't do much about for a while. She's pretty good, if Alice ever wants to see someone."

"She won't," Adrianna said.

"I know. I talked to Rayne. Her sister's really nice. It would be better if they could actually be there for each other more."

Adrianna nodded, not sure what else to say and Sarah did nothing to fill the silence. She was soon on her phone, Adrianna glancing over to see that she was texting Wyatt to tell him she was done. Adrianna ran her thumb over the screen of her phone in her pocket, but didn't bring it out and instead took her leave and went back to the dorm. She needed to get back to research and figure out something to help Lance get back to himself.

Alice was on her feet and by the mirror when Adrianna let herself back in. She could see the crack where Wonderland stared back at them. Alice had a hand on it, her fingers dipping into the hole in Wonderland and the rest of her fingers resting on the glass. The longing, so sad as she stared back into it, and her lips were moving and speaking words that Adrianna couldn't hear.

"Alice," Adrianna said quietly, trying not to startle her.

Alice snapped her attention back up, turning around and pulling her hand back. With her attention broken, the cracks to Wonderland sealed back up again, though Adrianna thought she could see someone standing on the other side.

"Sorry," Alice said. She looked like she wanted to say more, but her words died when she looked back at the mirror to find the crack gone.

"Are you okay?"

"I think so." There was a sour look that spread across Alice's face for only a moment before she smoothed it over. "Did you want a different book? The green one has a lot of dispelling stuff, so it might have something."

Adrianna let her change the subject, thinking back to what Sarah had said. Her mind was now spinning, wondering if tomorrow was a good idea. But it was way too late, and the thought of having to spend time with Arthur on her own worried her.

One thing at a time. And the next thing was to try to get her brother back.

CHAPTER 9

Skating

ADRIANNA ALMOST WISHED she didn't have to go see Sarah, but Alice was darker than she was and insisted that her makeup wouldn't match her properly. Alice wasn't doing anything to get herself ready, not at all concerned with what was about to happen or nervous about what Lance would think of her. She didn't understand why Adrianna was bothering with it either if she didn't like Arthur.

Adrianna didn't have an answer for that. They were meeting them off campus and she wanted to be pretty, so she went to Sarah hoping she had something in her color. Sarah handed her a few items and sent her back to Alice, wishing her luck and reminding her she wanted nothing to do with anything that was about to happen. Alice tried to help her apply everything, though her nonchalance about what was about to happen somehow made Adrianna more nervous.

They had to travel further out than expected, out into a community center in Seattle proper. Alice and Adrianna continued to try to come up with some plan the whole way there. Neither of them had found anything that would help free Lance and nothing else came up in the long drive into the city.

Adrianna had only agreed to a single date, at least, so they only needed to do enough here that she survived without being pressured into a second one. That would be simple enough on one condition. Arthur had to be far enough away from Lance and Alice so he couldn't do anything to threaten her into agreeing to anything new. They decided that Alice would get Lance away when necessary, if only so he couldn't be used against her when Arthur might try to pressure her again.

They stopped at the address and found themselves at a skating rink. Adrianna felt a pulse of excitement about it go through her, like this might not be so bad. She hadn't been skating in a few years and she was more than a little excited to get back on the ice again.

That was quickly countered with suspicion. She didn't know how Arthur would know she would enjoy this. Lance was there to give him all the information he might need about her, true, but Lance wasn't the one in control right now. Could the ghost read her brother's mind or compel him to talk? She didn't know and she wasn't sure she would like the answer.

"Hey, you made it," Arthur said, greeting them at the door as they made their way in. Thankfully, there were a lot of other people here. At first she was worried that it was a setup, that he rented out the whole space for just the four of them, but there were kids running around and plenty of adults watching their kids. There were even other teens their own age that could keep an eye out for anything strange that might happen. And she was wary of something strange happening.

Arthur didn't have the air of cockiness he normally did today. The way he smiled made her almost forget his successful attempts to blackmail her. Adrianna hoped this meant that he was going to at least try to make this nice and they could go back with no hard feelings. Maybe he would even let Lance go when they were done. She didn't want to see him again after this, no matter how much he would try to charm her to do it.

She tried to remind herself that he was having a hard time and that he had lost his entire world. That he had lost his hand and he had no one who understood him. And that was why he was kidnapping her brother. So that he could have his old friend back and one person familiar to him while he was here and trying to figure out his new life. A friend he didn't mind inflicting pain on when it served his purposes.

But maybe he would be nice today. And she could try to enjoy herself at least a little.

"Hey," she said. "Skating?"

"I heard you hadn't been in a while. Shall we?"

He led the way to get them skates, trailed by Lance while Alice and Adrianna followed behind. They got their skates and went to put them on. Something had changed in Arthur and he seemed a lot different now, though maybe it was only pity as she watched him struggle to get his laces done up with one hand. Part of her wanted to help him, but another couldn't forget that she was blackmailed into being here in the first place. It didn't matter how he smiled at her or how that smile made her feel; he was still holding her brother hostage.

"Everything okay?" Arthur asked as her eyes trailed back. He looked behind them and let out a little laugh. "It looks like Lance can handle it," he said, urging her onward toward the rink.

Behind her, Lance was helping Alice to her feet. She was flushed and embarrassed, unable to properly balance. It occurred to her that she hadn't ever asked Alice if she could skate, too in her own head about what had happened and what she would do with Arthur and her brother. Alice looked uncomfortable while Lance put his arm around her and helped her walk to the rink.

She could hear him promising to help her and another twinge of discomfort hit her. That wasn't her brother in there. It was some ghost she had seen palling around with

Arthur and not letting Lance see the light of day while he was around. She knew her brother wouldn't do anything Alice was uncomfortable with, but she had no idea about the ghost, no matter how Lance might seem to think he was fine.

Sarah's accusations came back to her. That Alice wasn't ready for something like this. That Adrianna shouldn't be making her do this and that Alice was only okay with it because Adrianna had asked her. She had promised it was only for this once and Alice would be free of any future obligation, but now that she watched she worried that this once was still too much to ask.

Arthur took her by the hand and smiled, leading her gently to the ice. She looked back at Alice, but she looked like she was doing all right. At the very least, it looked like Lance wasn't doing anything she needed to worry about. So long as she made it onto the ice soon after them, it would be fine and she would not protest. She could check in with her soon.

Adrianna hit the ice and could feel every groove in it under her not properly sharpened blade, knowing exactly where someone else had skated before and who had not learned how to stop properly, leaving dents and holes in the ice. It was a nostalgic feeling and she couldn't help but smile, testing herself out and trying to remember what she once learned how to do. She skated past Arthur and around several smaller children, finding it sounded much more busy than it was. Looking around, it looked like there was a second rink for hockey where a lot of the people outside were actually heading, leaving the free skate for people to enjoy the ice with children and people who were there to show off.

Arthur let her go at first, catching up after she slowed down and stopped herself from trying a jump. There was something fun about it, about gliding across the ice and feeling the wind in her hair, of weaving around the kids like a little obstacle course and watching them smile back as she passed them. It had been years since she had done anything like this. She wanted to play hockey to be with her brothers, but she was soon taken out when she was checked into the boards a little too hard and she got scared of it happening again. Yet she could still remember how to glide and turn and she wondered how much else.

"You're not half bad," Arthur said, though she could tell he was more impressed. He was watching her and he had been the whole time. "Where did you learn to do that?"

"It's been a while," Adrianna said. "I'm out of practice."

"It doesn't show."

Adrianna smiled, but her eyes drifted back to the place where people were just getting on the ice. She could see Lance and Alice, Alice on the wall and clinging for dear life while Lance hovered over her and ready to catch her when she fell. And it was definitely a when rather than an if.

"Hang on," she said, skating back towards her. There was a metal bar stranded in the middle of the rink, abandoned by whatever child was supposed to be using it and no other person in sight who looked like they might want it. Adrianna grabbed it as she headed back to Alice, going past Lance to talk to her and get her settled on it. "Hey," she said. "Here, you look like you could use this."

Alice looked up from clinging to the wall, looking flushed with embarrassment and effort from trying to keep her balance. Behind her, in the dim reflection of the windows, she could see Wonderland cracking through and peer in. Alice's eyes went to the bar, confused. "I'm okay," she said. "What's that?"

"It's a skate bar," Adrianna told her gently. "You can use it so you don't fall."

"Falling is not so bad so long as the landing is on something pleasant," Alice mused. "And I should say the ice would be most pleasant for me after a few moments. Though I suppose a gift to prevent me from earning that something pleasant might be a much better tactic to play upon. Thank you."

"That other world really is in your head, isn't it?" Lance asked in a way that made Adrianna very certain that Lance wasn't in there at all.

"Rude of you to mention it," Alice said, grinning as she finally got off the wall. She stumbled again on the ice, but Lance was there for her, less as a date and more like he was caring for a younger sister. She breathed a sigh of relief at the sight, comfortable at least that he wouldn't try to do anything to her. She hoped.

Arthur was back behind her soon enough and there was a glimpse of something else on his face before it went back to the gentle concern. It was only a flash of annoyance that might have flared up into anger if she waited any longer to get back to him. He earned himself a quick glare from Lance, and stayed quiet about whatever might have been going through his head. Instead, he took a moment to glare back before he spoke. "Everything all right over here?"

"Just getting her ice legs," Lance said. "We got it now, I think." There was something in the way he was looking at Arthur and how he spoke, that edge to his voice, that kept Arthur from saying anything else for the moment. Still, she could almost catch how Arthur was looking at Alice, like it pained him to keep whatever was in his head silent. Whatever it was, he held it in and they stayed together for now, in a flock around Alice as they moved around the rink.

"Have you really never been skating?" Adrianna asked, surprised. Alice had always been full of surprising things she could do. It was strange to encounter something that she couldn't for once.

Alice shook her head, gripping the bar hard and plodding

along slowly with more confidence. "I never really got to do a lot," she said as she stumbled. "It's okay, you guys can head off if you want," she insisted, quietly urging her to go off. They had a plan and she could handle this. And Lance, it seemed, wouldn't do anything terrible to her.

Arthur led them away and Adrianna let the conversation continue as they did laps, passing Alice and Lance several times. The topics started off safe, asking about classes and how Arthur was adjusting to school, and drifting into something more personal. He asked about her family, which seemed hollow to her given what he'd already learned about her and how.

"You can ask Lance about all of this," Adrianna said. She was feeling a little better about Arthur, more willing to give him a chance now that he wasn't actively tormenting her brother to make her pay attention to him. It was time for her to ask a few questions. "Where are you staying during the holidays? You don't have any family."

"I dealt with it," he said, waving his left arm, the sleeve pinned over where his hand would be. He looked like he'd forgotten it was missing. Even as he was trying so hard to be right handed, she noticed he kept trying to reach back for her with his left. It made it easy for her to skate out of the way casually so she wouldn't have to hold his hand, but she wanted to know more.

"And tuition?"

"Taken care of," he said cryptically. "I only started here with nothing. And it's not the first time. I know how to rebuild myself from nothing if I need to."

"What happened the first time?" she asked.

"I was chosen to be King," Arthur said wistfully. "Though I don't think I'll be getting that kind of luck here. I am sure even if you had kings that were chosen like I was, my sister would have done something to stop me now that she knows she didn't finish me off."

That was something that gave Adrianna pause for a lot of reasons. She wasn't sure where to start with any of that. With the fact that he was chosen as king? That he considered that as starting from nothing and working his way up? That he sounded bitter that he wouldn't be able to do it again while he was so very sure he could do it now without whatever thing was around to just hand him a kingship?

"Sister?" she asked first. It slipped out more than she had chosen it, but it seemed like a good starting point.

Arthur checked his phone before shrugging and looking back at her, tucking it back in his pocket. "Besides Alice, she's the one who put me here," he said. "She tried to kill me. Killed all of her sisters and my mentor. But I didn't die and it looks like neither did she, though she still froze my land solid and killed everyone on the island just to spite me."

"Wait," Adrianna said, trying to keep up with what she was being told. "So you were king. Of an island."

"The island was just in the kingdom. Avalon."

"Avalon," she said, though she wasn't sure what Avalon was, if it were the island or the kingdom. "And your sister froze the whole island solid? Along with your other sisters and your mentor and you."

"Oh, no. They weren't my sisters."

"But..." Adrianna started, but stopped. This was already a lot of information and she would need more of it to make everything make a lot more sense. "You were a king before you came here? And you've just decided to go to school instead of going back to your kingdom?" It seemed like a downgrade and one that he didn't necessarily have to do. If he could just tell Alice where he was from, she could get him back. Or, if she could figure out the white book, she could return him herself.

"There is no going back," Arthur told her. "She destroyed it all. It's in pieces now, shattered. There's no way to get back now. And besides," he said, turning back to look at her. Gently he touched her arms to bring her to a stop and gently brushed a stray hair out of her face. "I've found something worth staying for."

Her heart was racing as she stared back into those eyes and the breath was harder to come by. She thought she could fall into them, and she couldn't remember what it was she had been so hesitant about in that moment. He'd been nothing but nice to her, but there was something else here. If he kept touching her cheek like that, tucking her hair behind her ear, she might just...

And then he moved away, a gentle smile on his face and stopping before anything else might happen. She blushed furiously at where her mind was traveling, remembering they were in the middle of a skating rink with people around. She looked around madly, trying to tell if anyone was watching and she caught a few smiles and eyes pointed their way, and looking away as she watched them.

Taking another deep breath, she couldn't think of anything else she wanted to say in that moment and looked back around. Maybe now would be a good moment to try to bring them back to Alice, to make sure she was okay. What she found instead was that there was a skate bar that had been abandoned and neither Lance or Alice anywhere in sight.

"Where are they?" she asked, looking back and around for them. Maybe they had slipped into the rafters, but she also didn't see any cracks of Wonderland showing up in the glass anymore. She turned back to Arthur, still flustered but remembering now. This was the plan. Alice would get him away and try something to get the spirit out, or at least to let him be himself for a little while. Keep him away so Arthur couldn't use him against her. They were *supposed* to be gone.

Arthur pulled out his phone and scrolled through, Adrianna coming around to look at what was written on it. "Lance said that Alice was wandering off so he went to make sure she was okay. Apparently she can walk on her skates now, though. They'll meet up with us later."

Adrianna felt her own pocket vibrate and fished out her phone. Lance had left several messages telling her the same thing, though there were several more waiting for her that didn't make it to Arthur.

Lance

Claudia's in the mirror

She wants Alice

Following

Don't wait up

CHAPTER 10

Answer the Call

LANCE GRABBED ALICE by the shoulder and pulled her around to face him. She fell forward, her head spinning and everything around her feeling strange. Lance caught her before she could fall too far. She was still on the blades and it was significantly warmer here than it had been on the ice rink. It was also a lot darker and her heart was pounding hard, racing and very aware that something had happened. And, from the way Lance was gripping her shoulder as he tried to get her back on her feet, she knew it was pretty bad.

"Alice," he hissed, his voice quiet and unlike it had been a moment ago. "Alice wake up!"

"I'm awake," Alice said, unsteady on her feet and wavering. She reached out for something to hold onto, but Lance was the only thing there and she clung to him instead as she looked around. She knew the smell before she knew anything else about what was going on, and she was very aware that she was going to be in a lot of trouble. It wasn't so much musty as it was that the herbs made it feel musty. The stone walls were more of a giveaway than anything, showing that they were now in a castle decorated with rich reds and whites. In one direction, the hall was dark and Alice knew that was the part of the castle that had plunged itself into Neverland. "Why are we here?"

"Because you decided to disappear and walk into the smallest crack of a mirror," Lance hissed back at her, trying to both keep his voice down and to give an explanation. He was angry, but held her tightly anyway to keep her upright. She tried to pull herself away and he let go, pulling his hands away as if suddenly aware of what he was doing. She felt guilty for getting him into this, even if this had been essentially the plan. To get him away from Arthur so he could be himself and Alice could try to figure out one of the spells to get him away from him for good. It wasn't working like she'd hoped, but he was definitely away from Arthur now, and getting the chance to be himself. She thought it would take longer for the ghost to leave, but apparently not. All it took was a jaunt across the mirror.

But this was Wonderland. She could feel it running through her veins and in her heart beating ever so happily in her chest to be back. Even if she was in danger. Even if this was the absolute worst part of Wonderland she could possibly be in right now. At least she was here.

Alice only stayed balanced for part of a second before she promptly let herself fall on the ground. "Not so nice without the ice to break my fall," she muttered, going at the laces keeping the skates on. "I can't very well deal with whatever brought me here with these on. But if Wonderland has finally decided to stop listening to that Caterpillar—"

"*You* were the one who walked across," Lance insisted. "Claudia was there and you just waltzed through a crack in the mirror and then *he* decided that you needed someone to watch your back. And then he decided to up and *leave me here*."

"Well, I'm glad to have you," Alice said. "I mean, Adam would have been much better. He would be a little more willing to pull a knife on someone and run them through if they were too terribly inappropriate. But you will also do. Perhaps they will think you're him and it will work out about the same."

"Alice!"

"Yes?" she asked, discarding the skates and getting back up onto socked feet. She regarded the small pile and frowned. "Do you think they will be very mad if I don't return these? I suppose so long as my father doesn't decide to…"

At the mention of her father, a part of the spell cracked and she realized what was happening. She was going to be in so much trouble if she wasn't back in time for class tomorrow. It was Sunday already. If she didn't return from being off campus, they would call her father. And she would never be allowed back again. She might even be locked away for her disobedience. She probably wasn't supposed to be out with boys on the weekends. She should be studying and getting her grades up.

But she was here now. She was finally back. And it seemed that she had someone to thank for that. "Did you say Claudia?" she asked, wandering the other way down the hall. "She goes by Morgana now."

"She…" Lance let the question drop, tearing his skates off his feet and trying to keep up with Alice as she walked down the hall. "We need to get out of here. Where's a mirror?"

"This way," Alice said, continuing to meander through the hall. Lance didn't have to be here, but Alice didn't want to leave. She knew she should. They would notice her gone. It was Sunday. On Monday she needed to go to class or she would be missed. But she wanted so badly to stay for just a little longer, to see what had happened while she was gone.

And besides, she didn't actually know if she could go back. The thought made her smile.

She heard a clatter from behind one of the doors and stopped at it, tilting her head as she looked it over. It looked much like every other door in the hall, but this one was cracked open, letting out a steady stream of smoke that smelled heavily of herbs. It felt like there was someone looking for her on the other side. And, though she knew she shouldn't, she didn't know where else to go. She hadn't been planning to do this today. She had been planning to make herself fall in love. And she much preferred finding out who was trying to bring her into Wonderland instead and thank them for succeeding before she went looking for a way to get Lance back to school.

Since the door had already cracked itself open, she saw no problem with letting the crack drift open a little further so that she could better see what was inside, and what was inside was a little strange, even for Wonderland. The furniture had been either removed or pushed to the side, and the centre of the room was now dominated by a very intricate pattern, one that looked like every line had been drawn very intentionally in something different. It was made up of bones and wood, of smears of things that Alice didn't recognize and ones she did and would much rather never think about. The smell was strange, a husky and sour one covered by the sweet herbs hung high above her.

At the other side of the room standing at the edge of the circle on the floor, a woman stared at a mirror that Alice thought at first that she had set on fire. When she looked closer, it appeared that it was only incense at the top that had been set aflame. The woman had not seen Alice yet and Alice thought it was most rude that she had not acknowledged her. She knew she might have been distracted, but she had a guest, and guests must always be greeted when they were entering. Alice had been so cordial as to make sure she was quiet as to not cause a disruption. Though perhaps it was her who had been rude given that she had not announced herself when she entered. Alice opened her mouth to apologize when the woman turned muttering quietly to herself.

That was Morgana. The look of surprise was even like Adrianna's, despite the older features on her face. "So it did work," she said, more to herself than to Alice. "How long have you been there? Is that..."

Alice looked behind her to see Lance was there lingering over her shoulder. He was staring at Morgana as she swept across the room to the pair of them, her attention squarely on him. "You boys really do have to get into everything, don't you?" she asked, a smile tugging at her lips. The expression suddenly soured as she peered at him. "What are you doing here?" she asked, the friendly tone vanishing.

"I..." Lance faltered before regaining himself again. He didn't like anything happening right now, that much was clear, and he took a sudden step away, trying very hard not to look at Morgana's neckline that was now directly in front of him. "I should be asking you that," he said. "You just left and—"

"Not you," she said, waving a casual hand. All in a

moment, Lance's whole demeanor changed. His stance shifted and his shoulders broadened, his head sitting straighter on his neck and his face contorting into something less scared and more displeased. "Lancelot," Morgana said. "You've returned to me."

"Not by choice," Lance told her. "You're doing something."

"As are you," Morgana observed, looking down at the skates. She looked back, seeing Alice's socked feet and pondered. "I've interrupted something, haven't I? She's a bit young for you."

"We both know she is," he told her. "I don't know what you're trying to do here, but you need to stop. You've done more than enough already. There's no point in hurting children to do whatever you're planning to do."

"And what do you think I'm trying to do?" she asked. It occurred to Alice that this was a lot nicer than when Arthur was talking to her. "If you don't want to be here, you can leave. In fact," she said, turning to him with a smile. "I can let you go myself, if that's what you desire. I could give you your afterlife at last."

"You'd hurt the boy."

Morgana made a laugh and cupped his face, smiling at him. "He was my child for a time. You are safe from me while you wear his face. Or your own. Spirits are different matters, and yours is more chained than entangled to this world. It wouldn't be hard to move it along to the—"

Lance grabbed her hand and shoved it away. "I'm staying here," he said firmly. "Your brother has gone mad since you tried to kill him. I need to make sure he doesn't do anything rash."

Morgana looked offended for only a moment before she backed away. Lance tried to move, but his feet didn't listen and remained firmly on the ground. Morgana cordially decided that they were done for the moment, at least. He fought to break free, but still he stood right where she left him, mouth opening to say more but no words coming out of him. Slowly, whatever kept his feet in place moved up, more and more of him growing still though he continued to try to break free.

Alice wondered what they were talking about, but she didn't get a chance to ask. Morgana swept down to her and Alice found that she couldn't move either.

"Then we just have the small matter to finish before I can send you back along your way," Morgana said. She looked at Alice with a gracious smile. There was some measure of affection there but it was much more the look of a cat as she was about to finally claim a particularly difficult to catch mouse. "This may hurt," she said.

"Then perhaps you should consider not—"

Alice didn't know what she had been expecting, but Morgana shoving her hand directly into her chest was not it. Her eyes went wide as she felt her reach deep inside her chest and wrap her fingers around her now pounding heart and gave it a squeeze. Whatever sound she wanted to make caught in her throat, too stunned that it was happening at all to register pain or anything else.

There was a swift pull and there was nothing else. The last thing she saw was a heart — her own heart — beating in someone else's hands.

Chapter 11

Problem Solving

ALICE WAS IN bed Monday morning as if she had never disappeared at all. Adrianna thought she heard the door and saw a flash of purple, but she had been more asleep than awake and wasn't sure if she had seen anything. She was grateful, at least, that she was back before classes. Disappearing on a Sunday was dangerous and typically not what Alice would do. More concerning was that Lance had followed her across, but they both appeared to be back and neither of them looked worse from the experience. At least, they didn't have any visible injuries.

There was something different about Alice when she got up, but she couldn't put her finger on it. She wasn't sure Alice could either, noting moments of confusion that crossed her face before she settled a little too easily into that guarded calm that was so normal for her. Still, Adrianna would question it another time. They had to get to class.

"What happened yesterday?" Adrianna asked as they made their way to class, both having slept in too late to grab a proper breakfast. They dashed through the cafeteria to grab muffins in hopes they wouldn't be late. "Were you okay?"

"I'm... fine," Alice said, looking almost confused about it.

"What happened?"

"I'll tell you later," Alice said. "What about you? I'm sorry I left you there with him. How was the rest of it?"

Adrianna shrugged, blushing and looking down at her muffin as they went up the busy stairs to class. "It was kind of okay," she admitted. "I mean, he still sucks. He is using his friend to possess Lance and Adam doesn't trust him. But, I mean, Adam *did* try to throw him at the Bandersnatch and he was willing to let you die too, so he's probably not the best person to go by."

"Adam's just worried about Tiger Lily and mad that I wouldn't let him go back to see her again," Alice told her with a shrug. "So not all his fault either. But he *does* still have Lance possessed by a ghost that doesn't want to be there."

"And he's not nice to you."

Alice shrugged. "I wasn't nice to him either," she said. "I haven't been nice to a lot of people."

It might have been a good time to give her a hug, Adrianna thought, if they weren't about to walk into class. Instead, they took their seats, Adrianna a little ways down from Alice. They were alphabetical, which kept them from comparing notes about yesterday. Worse, Alice didn't use her phone in class and that meant that she couldn't continue this conversation in text during the lecture.

Her phone buzzed while the teacher spoke at the front of the room and she checked it under the table, placing it in her lap while she took notes. Kevin was a couple rows in front of her with Heather and had questions in their group chat.

Kevin

You got in so late. He didn't kill you?

Heather

Didn't even see Alice come in ;)

Adrianna

We'll tell you about it at lunch

Adrianna tried her best to focus on class, but her mind was already spinning with how to deal with it. She couldn't just tell them that Alice had vanished, but she hadn't talked to her enough to know how to work around it. Worse, she didn't even have her next class with Alice, so there would be no way for her to try and work out what to say with her. It was probably best to come up with something generic. Or maybe she could just try not to say anything and hope they wouldn't press her about what Alice was doing yesterday.

Alice was so much better at this than she was.

Still, she knew Alice wasn't what they would ask her about. They would ask about Arthur and that was a much more difficult question for her to answer. If she was honest, it was nice and he was charming and fun to be around. But she didn't like him and she could never forget what he was doing to her family. She would not be doing it again. She fulfilled her part of the bargain.

She hoped. If he threatened Lance again, she would probably cave and do whatever he asked. And it wouldn't take long before he would use him against her again to make her continue to give him a chance.

"Alice."

Adrianna broke out of her reverie as the teacher called on Alice. Mr. David never called on anyone unless they offered their hand, and Alice *never* offered her hand in any class, no matter how well she knew the material. But looking over — and she knew she wasn't the only one looking — Alice lowered her hand and talked about the causes of World War I. Adrianna didn't even look at her notes, staring down at her lap and seeing the messages flying past in all caps demanding to know what was going on with Alice.

Heather

ADDIE

ADDIE

WHAT HAPPENED

DID YOU REPLACE HER

IN FIVE YEARS

FIVE YEARS

SHE HAS NEVER SPOKEN WILLINGLY IN CLASS

FIVE YEARS

I THOUGHT CLASS MADE HER MUTE

ADDIE

WHAT IS THIS

Sarah

Omfg you guys what is going on

Heather

ALICE

SHE ANSWERED A QUESTION

IN CLASS

Robert

So?

She knows shit

Heather

SHE ROSE HER HAND FOR THIS

Robert

...

Adrianna

You know she's going to read these later

Kevin

Hey Alice

Heather

ALICE

WHAT HAPPENED YESTERDAY

DID YOU GET LAID

ARE YOU A CLONE

WHAT IS THIS

Sarah

Alice never checks her phone

Robert

She probably will this time

Heather

I HAVE MANY QUESTIONS

IF YOU COULD MAKE HER CHECK THEM NOW
THAT WOULD HELP

ADDIE

WORK YOUR MAGIC

MAKE HER DO THINGS

Heather shot a look back at her and Adrianna took a breath. This was too much for right now. She took her phone off of her lap and placed it face down on the desk beside her to show she was no longer paying attention to the string of messages. She would deal with this later. For right now, class was less complicated. Even if class also had a strange version of Alice.

Throughout class, Adrianna kept looking up to see Alice looking perfectly normal. Wyatt was next to her and he didn't seem to think there was anything to be worried about, but even he looked surprised when she turned to ask him about something. Alice rarely spoke at all during class. None of this was normal for her, but she didn't look any different than before. It wasn't like Lance. She still held herself the same, still spoke the same when she spoke at all. Adrianna wanted to ask him later what he thought, but there was no way to do so that didn't seem awkward. She picked up the phone, ignoring the stream in the group chat to message Wyatt, but he didn't respond.

In her next class, Heather sent a few hurried messages, confirming that there was indeed something different about Alice but that this was probably a good thing. She asked Lance and he confirmed that they had not slept together and Heather needed to get her head out of the toilet. She wondered what exactly she'd asked to get that response, but decided it was best not to ask.

She narrowly avoided answering any of Heather's rapid-fire questions about what happened yesterday with her. She was curious about what Arthur was like, but Adrianna dodged the requests for information by virtue of putting her phone on the desk and relying on the quiet of Math until it was over.

They found Sarah and Alice at Sarah's locker on the way to the cafeteria and stopped to join them there. "Hey," Adrianna said, looking from Sarah to Alice, Alice looking just like she usually did as she adjusted her backpack on her back. "How was Lit?"

"Dull," Sarah said.

"Apparently there was a bet?" Alice asked, smiling at Adrianna like she wanted her to do the same. "About whether or not I slept with Lance?"

"I had nothing to do with that," Adrianna said. "Are you okay?"

Alice shrugged. "Why wouldn't I be?" she asked. It took her a moment before Sarah nudged her, giving her a look before she looked back to her locker. She might not want to get involved any more, but she was doing something now. Adrianna shot her a look, silently asking for answers.

"She hasn't told me," Sarah said. "I told her not to. Not my business. Not getting involved in this stuff anymore. I'm going ahead, you two get your story about yesterday straight. I'll see you in the cafeteria in a bit."

"Oh, I'm not letting you guys get away with that," Heather said, looping her arms in both Alice and Adrianna's. "I leave you guys alone for too long, Alice might teach you how to *not* tell me what happened. And I'm not having any of that." She laughed and brought them down to the cafeteria with her.

Sarah rolled her eyes at the sight of them rushing to join her, but did nothing to stop them. They got lunch and sat down at a table at the cafeteria, finding Kevin and Adam saving one for them. They took seats around it, Adrianna staying close to Alice to keep an eye on her.

Alice frowned at her bag as she shrugged it off and it fell to the ground with a much heavier thud than it usually did. Normally she had nothing in it, using it as a prop so she could pull things out of it and only bringing enough for one class at a time. Now it looked just as full as everyone else's.

"So," Kevin asked finally when no one else brought it up, leaning across the table to Adrianna. "Arthur's still a dick, right?"

"He was actually pretty nice," Adrianna conceded. "And charming and everything. I had a good time."

"But…?"

"Never again."

"Good," Heather said, glaring across the cafeteria. "He's still a pain in my ass, so I wouldn't want to deal with him more than I have to."

Adrianna laughed at that, relaxing into her seat as the attention turned back to Alice. At least, Heather's did. "And

I'm guessing *you* had a good time," Heather said, looking meaningfully at Alice.

"Yeah."

"So?"

Alice looked at her. "So?"

"You going to see him again?"

"I'm seeing him right now," Alice pointed out. "He's right behind you."

Sure enough, Heather looked back and both Arthur and Lance were coming for their table, both looking entirely obnoxious. Arthur looked down to Adrianna, flashing that beautiful smile. "You miss me?" he asked, looking like he intended to sit down. Next to her, Sarah slid her tray closer to remove the space he might have tried to force himself into.

Next to her, Lance leaned in to say something quietly to Alice. She nodded and got up, vacating her seat and following him away without so much as looking back at her lunch. Arthur smoothly slipped into her chair after she left, smiling and looking entirely too charming as he settled in.

Heather was in shock when Alice left, almost to the point where she didn't notice that Arthur was there. Adam more than made up for it, obviously furious to see Arthur so close to his sister. He glared daggers at him as he got in closer and Adrianna was happy he had nothing sharp in arm's reach.

"She didn't say yes," Adam said as Arthur looked smugly across the table at him.

"And I don't recall her saying no," Arthur said. "Now be a good boy and let us have a nice chat, would you?"

Adam flushed red. Adrianna remembered being told about a time Arthur turned him into a dog. Now, Arthur played with his fingers, looking like he might do it again if he wanted. Adam backed down, a growl emanating from deep in the back of his throat at Heather groaned and glared at him.

"What do you want, Arthur?" she asked.

"Can't a guy say hello to his girl between classes?" he asked. "I wanted to see how you felt about getting lunch together."

"We went out once," Adrianna said cautiously, eyeing those fingers and how they played on themselves. Adam might be thinking about how he had been turned into a dog before, but Adrianna was thinking about all the other things he could do with that hand. Gently she reached over and put her hand over it, pressing it down onto the table. She realized the gesture could easily be mistaken for affection and not a plea for him to stop threatening her family, but she didn't know what else to do. "It was only once."

"And yet," Arthur said, turning his palm over to hold her hand. Adrianna hesitated before she let it happen. If he wasn't doing things with his fingers, then he wasn't doing anything that could hurt anyone, at least. "Here we are." He leaned over to whisper something in her ear.

"Don't worry. I'll even let your brother go now that I have you."

Adrianna felt her blood run cold. She didn't like what was happening. He'd agreed to let Lance go, but something about that made her sure that there was something more. Like he was only safe so long as she was compliant. It wasn't what he said, but she couldn't know what he meant by it, if those eyes and that smile were being kind or trying to coerce her again. He was still making her heart flutter with both terror and attraction. And she hated all of it.

"Do you have to do this right here?" Kevin asked.

"I'll think about it," Adrianna said. She pulled herself out of his hand, getting to her feet and walking away from the table. "Excuse me, I have to... I'll be back."

She felt breathless when she left, not sure what she was thinking. Was he even telling the truth? It sounded too good to be true, and yet like something he could reverse as soon as she did something he didn't like. She was both attracted to him and wanted nothing to do with him all at once, and she could recognize that he was threatening her to keep her in his company. It was wrong. She had no guarantees. She should say no.

But instead she went to find out where Alice had gone.

She and Lance had slipped off, leaving their food behind. It was probably good, meaning that Adrianna could finally ask her about what happened yesterday.

She found the two of them talking quietly in the hall outside, sitting next to one another on a windowsill. They hushed their conversation and Lance was not himself but the ghost. There was something else happening here, something that she didn't want to get too involved in, but she smiled at seeing how close they were. There was a moment as she approached, where the other Lance stepped in and grabbed Alice's hand, looking her in the eye and saying something. It felt strangely intimate.

Adrianna almost didn't want to interrupt, but she needed to find out what was going on. What had happened last night. And what she needed to do now. She walked wide enough around them that they would see her coming. She waited for them to notice her before she approached. Abruptly, Lance looked down at their hands and let go of Alice, though it was too late. She had seen. And she didn't know what it meant.

"Alice, what's going on?" Adrianna asked. "Lance? What... I don't know where to start. Where did you go yesterday?"

Alice looked at her a moment and softened as she told her. She didn't look around this time before she spoke. "Wonderland," she said. "I'm sorry, it just kind of happened."

"I'll say," Lance said. The ghost version of him looked ready to roll his eyes at her for being so indifferent about the matter.

"Is everything okay over there?" she asked. "You don't usually just go like that unless something bad happened."

"It's good," Alice told her. "It's all over now."

"Over?" Adrianna didn't know how to take that or what that meant. Over meant a lot of things.

"I don't have to go back anymore."

"Why not?"

"All the hearts are back," she said. "I put all the hearts back, so I'm done over there. Wonderland is all done and I can just focus on being here now."

Adrianna searched Alice's face for the lie, but it wasn't there. Alice smiled widely and Adrianna matched it, relief flooding through her. "It's really all over?" she asked, almost not wanting to believe it. "Alice that's great!" She cried, grabbing her up in a hug and squeezing her.

There was a hesitation to the hug as Alice pulled away, perhaps too quickly. But it was over. It was really over for her. She was free of that terrible place and she never had to go back again. This was the best thing that could possibly happen. "I can't believe you're done! And that you didn't tell me before!"

"We kind of slept in," she said. "I wanted to give it a bit of time."

"It's overwhelming," Adrianna said, coming back to her and holding her hands, giving her a squeeze. Alice wasn't much for hugs, she knew, so that was probably too much for her. "You didn't think you'd ever be able to do it, but you're done at last! I knew you could do it."

"I can't teleport anymore, though," she said. "I had to run back to our room to get my books for Lit."

Adrianna laughed. "You'll have to just bring everything with you like the rest of us," Adrianna said with a laugh. She took a breath and let out a happy sigh, letting her thoughts about Arthur fall away and the smile settling on her face to match Alice's. "I'm so happy for you."

Alice smiled. "Me too." She let out a breath and glanced back at Lance behind Adrianna before returning her eyes to Adrianna again. "I can't get the books out anymore, though. Everything I didn't do, it's not going to get done anymore."

Adrianna almost laughed. "I'll deal with the rest," she said, eyeing Lance. She had a way to get him free. It really was almost over.

"So what do you say we head back in there?" she asked. "Suffer the questioning about yesterday. Tolerate Arthur for just a little longer. Eat?"

Adrianna smiled and hooked her arm in Alice's, bringing her back into the cafeteria. She almost didn't notice that Lance didn't follow them. Something good had finally happened. She didn't have to worry about Alice anymore. She had a way to get Lance free. This whole nightmare was almost all over.

CHAPTER 12

Gossip

THERE ONCE WAS a beautiful island filled with trees and teeming with magic. On this island there lived five women, all of them happy and very much in love with the island and who cared deeply for each other. They were sisters, each with their own desires and goals and dreams. One had left the island and returned only recently, bringing back her heartbreak and stories of the world that she had left behind. Of a son that she loved so very much but who needed to find his own way, no matter how terrible his choices might be. Of a brother she loved perhaps too much. Of the knight she had loved perhaps too much. Of a mentor that she loved perhaps too much.

But that life she had left behind. Her sisters accepted her back to the island, and she was happy there, though she often found her mind wandering back to the mainland and to the things happening there. To the men she had loved. To the people she had left behind. She loved her sisters, but they did not know as much of the outside world as she did. She spoke mostly of the terrible parts and tried to convince herself it was all terrible. But in her heart, she wanted to see how they were doing. Maybe one last time, she wanted to see what had happened.

Her sisters did not try to stop her, but still she did not go. She feared she would want to stay if she left again, to live with the good when so much was so bad. So many horrible, terrible things waited for her out there. So much heartbreak and betrayal. She had done some of both herself, had learned jealousy and tasted revenge. Being here on the island, it scared her how much she had liked revenge.

And so she vowed she would never leave the island again. She missed the world of men, but she was better for being here. It was serene and untouched by their poison.

Or it was until that boat appeared on the horizon and she knew in her heart that she was about to see one of the men she missed so much again. Her heart was full and the longing melted away with hope and thoughts of what might come. Of anticipation. Of joy. She didn't have to leave her island to know what had become of them or to enjoy them again.

SO THIS WAS what being normal was like. No strange thoughts, no having to watch what she said, no looking longingly into the mirrors for something staring back at her. No responsibility of a whole other world weighing on her thoughts. There was only school and her social life to worry about now, and she didn't have much of a social life to begin with.

She could have done without the heavy bag, though. Rather than getting used to it, she could swear it was getting harder to carry around. How everyone else had done it so long, she didn't know. Naps were creeping into her life now just to recover from the effort of it all.

Well, that was one of the reasons.

Heather poked her awake. Alice yawned and looked around the table, seeing that they were the only two left. Heather had spread out more than just homework in front of her, her schedule and brightly colored notes from council also littering the table. There was a budget that included the word *bokken* and other bits of paper that looked suspiciously like they were from other clubs that she might have joined to fill more of her hours.

"Hey," she said, withdrawing her bright green highlighter and looking back through the textbook that she had directly in front of her. "Have you finished the paper yet? I need another set of eyes for mine."

"Sure," Alice said, gesturing for her to hand over her computer. Heather looked at her for a moment before she passed it over, pulling the plug on it as she did. The computer was a lot heavier than Alice's, older and louder, but Heather still managed to drag it with her everywhere. Alice placed it in front of her with a heavy clunk and started looking through the work.

"I could have just sent you the file," Heather told her, amusement tugging at her face.

"This is easier."

Words caught in Heather's throat and she covered them with a gentle laugh, pulling one of the other pages toward her to start poring through it. "Only a matter of time before Lance teaches you how to actually use a computer," she told her. "You guys are good together."

Alice nodded, adding a period here and correcting the spelling of a name there. Besides a few small typos, Alice had trouble finding anything that she needed to correct. But it was one of Heather's essays, and Heather was top of their class.

"I think he joined Combat Club because of you. I mean he's surprisingly good at it, but he didn't join until after you guys started going out. He keeps watching you, you know. Even when he's hanging out with Arthur."

"Does he?"

"Adam thinks there's something wrong with him," Heather continued. "He keeps saying that Lance isn't his brother anymore."

"He's not," Alice said. "Not when he's around Arthur, anyway."

"That's what he keeps saying. But he says it like that. Like there's something else going on."

"There is," Alice told her. "It's okay. It'll be over soon."

"Do all of you have to be so cryptic?"

"Yep." Alice smiled and turned the computer back to her. "It looks fine. I fixed a couple small things, but it really wasn'ta lot."

"One of these days you guys have to tell me what this secret club is all about," Heather told her as she took the computer back. "Sarah gets to know and she won't tell me about it either."

"You're busy and it's over," Alice said. "Nothing left to talk about."

"You *just* said it wasn't over yet." Heather's eyes narrowed on her. She looked around the room before she leaned in closer. "So you'll tell me about Lily?"

That caught Alice by surprise. "Lily?" she asked. She wasn't sure what to tell her or what she might already know about her. Adam didn't ever seem to want to talk about her, but Adam didn't want to talk to Alice much at all. She wasn't sure what Heather might already know or what Adam had already told her.

"Look, either you tell me about Lily or you tell me about Lance. And I can see all over your face that you don't want to talk about Lance. So tell me about this ex that Adam won't talk about."

A cough escaped her and Heather pulled out a bottle of water to hand to her. Alice accepted it with a grateful smile and drank. She'd missed Heather when she was like this. When she hadn't held herself back so strongly and when she acted like she wanted to be around Alice.

Alice placed the bottle between the two of them. "Lily's a friend," she started, trying to pick her words carefully. She couldn't talk about Wonderland, but she could talk about Tiger Lily as a person. "She's very independent. Strong, brave, a lot like you in a lot of ways. Always working really hard and trying to do the right thing."

"Pretty?"

"Yeah."

Alice wondered if she had said the wrong thing. Heather looked upset about that, not asking anything else for a very long moment. Emotions flickered rapidly across her face, from sadness to anger to something else that Alice couldn't place. When they stopped, a crease stayed in her forehead.

"And?" Heather pressed. A resigned look came over her. "Do you know why they didn't work?"

A tight smile pulled at Alice's lips. A version of the truth. "She decided that he should go home, even if he didn't want to."

"Sounds like she wasn't that interested."

Alice shrugged, but Heather looked a lot happier. She wondered if she'd said too much with how happy it made Heather, if she had somehow revealed something that she shouldn't have. But Alice didn't know the details of Adam and Tiger Lily's relationship or if it had ever existed.

Another cough bubbled out of Alice and she covered her mouth with one hand, reaching for the bottle of water with the other. She took another drink and Heather gestured for her to keep the bottle with her. "Are you getting sick?" Heather asked.

"I hope not."

Heather regarded her before getting to her feet. "Be right back," she said, excusing herself and heading to the wash-rooms.

Alice set the water bottle down next to her, opening her laptop and trying to remember what homework she had left. There was a reading for Lit, so she reached down into her backpack. Her fingers bumped into the books she had already put in there and Alice jumped, pulling her hand back.

Right. The book was upstairs. She couldn't just pull it out of her bag anymore.

Of everything she couldn't do, she missed the teleporting the most. Being able to send her hand far away to retrieve her books was amazing. Now she had to do what everyone else did and carry what she needed with her or forget it and hope she wouldn't need it.

She was not alone for long, Adam dropping his bag on the table and dropping into a seat next to her a moment later. He propped an elbow up on the table and rested his chin in it, staring at her. "So," he said. "I hear you're all done in Wonderland."

"Yep," Alice said.

"Forever?"

"Forever."

"Bullshit."

Alice adjusted the computer in front of her and Adam promptly closed it. "We're not done. There's no way you're *done* with Wonderland."

"And yet, here we are." Alice was tired as she returned his gaze. "I don't know what you want from me, Adam."

"How is Alice of Wonderland ever *done* with Wonderland, I wonder? Or did you just decide you'd had enough and gave up?"

"All the hearts are back," she told him. "Wonderland

doesn't need me for anything else. I'm not even part trea- cle anymore."

Adam's face grew redder the more she spoke and he seemed to get bigger the more Alice shrank away from him. "Don't lie to me, Alice. People are dying over there and you won't let me go back and help. There's no way you got all the hearts back and fixed the giant hole in the universe in an afternoon. *Especially* not with Lance. Or whatever he is now."

"Lance wasn't much help."

"Did he even let Lance out?" Adam asked, his tone cut- ting. "He won't let my brother out at all anymore. You know that's not even Lance fawning all over you, right?" He pulled himself back from saying whatever else he wanted to, look- ing around and sitting up. "I don't like it, but at least Addie's going to fix it."

Alice took another drink of water, feeling the tickle in the back of her throat coming back up again. "Is she?" she asked. "She didn't tell me."

"Arthur said he'd let Lance go so long as Addie kept going out with him. Since you won't do anything about it, that's what we're stuck with. We'll see if Lance still likes you when he's himself again."

Alice stayed very quiet, following Adam's eye line to where Heather reappeared. She let the two of them settle in next to one another and opened up her computer, quietly continuing to work and speaking only when spoken to. Heather still held no animosity, but she could feel the daggers being glared at her from Adam when she wasn't watching.

She was going to have to talk to Lance. He didn't seem to think Arthur could send him back, but she needed to be sure. She could not afford to let him go back to normal just yet.

CHAPTER 13

Facade

IT TOOK A lot longer to get ready in the morning now. Life might be more vibrant, classes more interesting, friendships less full of uncertainty and animosity, but there were costs to everything. Not that Alice was any stranger to doing what she needed to in order to keep a secret. It was just the first time she had to adjust her sleep schedule in order to conceal one.

She carefully made sure her sports bra covered the majority of the hole in her chest. She was never without one under her shirt now, just to make sure it maintained the shape under scrutiny. Even when she slept, she kept it on and tucked herself under layers of blankets so Adrianna wouldn't notice. And so far, it had been working. She worried about the warmer months and what she would do when she couldn't do that any longer. The collars would get lower and she would need to think of something that would keep her chest covered. But she didn't need to worry about that yet. If she was careful, she might not have to worry about that at all.

She bent this way and that to make sure it wouldn't show the concave part of her chest when she tripped or fell at club today. Her cough wasn't going away, and with it she found she was getting clumsier. She couldn't go to the nurse, not knowing how she might react to finding that Alice was walking around without her heart. Her life at school was just getting better. Heather was talking to her again. Everyone was. She couldn't be sent away now.

Out of the corner of her eye, she saw a flash of purple and she gathered her things. Adrianna was still asleep in their room and Alice moved quickly and quietly to leave her to it, heading off to Combat Club. With a book in hand and a sweater thrown over her head, she opened it and tried to finish off the chapter before she got to the club.

Peter fell in step next to her at some point along the walk. She hadn't heard him approach and wondered if he had been on his feet at all before he was next to her. He said nothing at first, Alice looking him over and noticed immediately the dark circles under his eyes. Kevin mentioned that he was having trouble sleeping and he was waking up in strange places. It was clearly taking a toll on him.

"Awfully rude to just show up without introduction," she said, a grin crossing her face. She closed the book, using a finger to mark the page.

He let out a laugh. "I heard you were done with all that," he said.

"Who said?"

"Adam. He looked pissed about it." He smiled back at her. "You don't have to lie to him, you know."

Alice opted to not correct him yet. As far as she was concerned, with her heart out she was done. There was nothing else she *could* do. She slipped the bit of paper she was using as a bookmark in place and looked him over. "You look awful," she said.

"Nice to see you too," he countered, though he didn't move away or look remotely offended at the accusation. "I gave up Neverland, but I keep trying to get there in my sleep. It's like it's calling me back. I don't know what's happening. My shadow already went without me." He lifted off the ground and drifted a few steps, wiggling his foot in the air.

Alice looked down at the ground, pushing down a cough and narrowing her eyes on it as if it would help. The morning was fairly bright, but she could spot her own shadow on the ground. It was faint, but it was there. Below Peter, there was nothing in all directions, despite the sun clearly shining down on them. He set his foot back on the ground.

"No one noticed yet," he said. "But one day I'm going to go to sleep and I'm going to wake up in Neverland, I know it."

"What are you going to do?"

"Not sleep," he said. "If I don't sleep, I don't have to wake up somewhere weird, right? Besides, I was reading this thing where a guy just slept for an hour at a time for years. I'm just going to do that until I stop waking up in weird places."

"That's *a* plan," Alice said as they reached the gym. "Good luck?"

Peter shrugged and looked like he was about to ask her something, but too soon they were amidst people. Alice was grateful for him letting it drop, and she hoped that he'd forget when they were done. For right now, she put her book on the side of the gym and took up a spot on the floor to start stretching before joining in on the warm ups.

Arthur and Adam were already at it, Adam bumping into him on his lap around and Arthur looking for retaliation. Alice hung well back from the pack, her lungs burning from just the first bit of the jog. She barely made it around once before she started coughing with every breath. She took a detour on the second lap to get a bottle of water.

"Hey," Heather said, running up to her. "Alice. Are you okay?"

"I'll be fine," Alice said, taking a breath in. She exhaled with several coughs, covering her mouth with her hand and feeling the cool air from her lungs pouring out around it. Her head was starting to spin, but she closed her eyes and forced herself to look forward. "It's just a cough. I'll be fine."

"You look terrible," Heather said. She looked around, her eyes falling on Lance and waving him closer. "Lance, can you take Alice to the back? You need to lie down for a bit, Alice. Have you eaten anything yet today?"

Alice shook her head, but that only made the world spin again.

"Lie down for a bit, then take her for something to eat," Heather instructed them. "Back room's open."

Alice didn't protest as Lance helped her into the back. "Are you okay?" he asked her quietly, not for the first time. He hovered over her more often now, both in Combat Club and out. This wasn't the first time he kept her from falling, but he sounded much more worried this time than he had before. "You're pale."

"I'm okay," Alice said. Lance helped her into the back room and sat her on the bed. There was nothing to be worried about. It happened now and then. "Just a little dizzy."

"That's happening more now," Lance told her. "You can't keep hiding this. They need to know. You can't live forever without your heart."

"But it's better now," Alice insisted. She coughed again.

"I'm obviously not dying without it. I'm just... just a little dizzy. You aren't going to say anything, right?"

Lance didn't look happy about the request. "I failed to protect you," he said. "I'll keep your secret for now. But you aren't well. And you're getting worse."

"I'll be fine," Alice insisted, another wave catching her now that she was still. "I just need to take it a little easy and I'll be... fine..."

She wasn't sure what was happening, but she wasn't able to keep upright anymore. She sagged forward as a wave of nausea washed over her and slipped off the side of the bed. The floor should have rushed up to meet her but it never did, Lance catching her again before she could hit the ground.

The wave passed and she looked up, seeing Lance holding her and looking at her like he was worried she was about to fade away. Alice offered a smile. "Thanks," she said. Behind him, Alice could see a blur of something else, but she didn't catch who it was. She decided it didn't matter, her vision now blurry and she couldn't quite focus on anything in front of her. "I'm okay."

"You aren't," Lance told her.

"Don't tell anyone."

He looked at her sternly and clearly hating every moment of this. "Not until you can't stop me."

Alice nodded and let him help her back up onto the bed.

She kept her eyes closed and head bowed, waiting for the nausea to pass. "You might not have much longer," she warned him. "Arthur's planning to let you free."

"He's already tried," Lance said. "He can only make me leave if I decide to."

"And you don't?"

"I have a debt to repay. Until you're no longer in danger, I'm not going anywhere." She opened her eyes to see him studying her. "You won't believe me, will you?" he asked. "You are very unwell, Alice. This is not good."

"I'm fine," she insisted.

In front of her, Lance shifted. Alice watched that annoyance shift to surprise then panic. He let out a heavy breath, mouth open to say something, but no words escaped from his mouth. His eyes searched her, hesitating and barely believing what he was seeing. That disbelief turned into determination and he turned away, sprinting for the door.

Lance made it three steps before his body shifted again, stopping in his tracks and standing up straight. His shoulders grew more broad and he turned back around, annoyance etched into his features.

A laugh echoed in the small room. "He thinks he can help someone who wishes only to be left alone," Cat said, appearing in the corner in the room. He was a purple haired boy today, holding a bright pink frozen drink in his hands and playing with the straw. "*And* he thinks a released prisoner will not try to run."

"What do you want, Cat?" Alice asked. The world wasn't moving so much anymore and her lungs didn't feel so deeply on fire anymore.

"You think you'll be happier without your heart," he said. "Perhaps you will spare yourself the pain when it breaks so far away from you, but you will soon realize that a girl without a heart is not a girl at all. Not for very long."

"I couldn't go back if I wanted to," she said. "And I don't want to. I'm done with Wonderland."

"Lies might protect you from your friends' questions, and perhaps even the truth for a time, but they will not protect you from everything," Cat said. "And you can always go back. You just can't use the mirrors any longer. Those are finally mine once more. So perhaps there isn't only bad that has come of this."

"You aren't helping," Lance snapped at him. He advanced on him and made a grab for the cup in his hands. "If you must stay, at least give her some of that drink."

"This is a feisty one," Cat said, everything below his neck vanishing. He appeared on the bed next to Alice, one arm draped over her shoulder and leaning in very close. "But he keeps your secrets better than a diary. The lock is hidden within his pages instead of without. All it takes is keeping a friend prisoner until it's much too late for you to be saved. And you can be saved, if only you would ask."

Alice didn't move away, even as his words became a quiet purr in her ear. His large purple eyes watched her, tempting her with the promise of rescue. In front of her, the sticky sweet smell of his drink tempted her, the straw lingering very close to her lips. He would help her, was already offering to help her, but she would have to take that help.

But she was fine. She was dizzy now and then, but she had not been eating enough lately. Her time was spent enjoying life as she was supposed to, without the headaches and her mind constantly on Wonderland. Her friends saw nothing wrong with her, and they would notice before anyone else.

She coughed as if the cough needed to remind her that it existed.

It was spring. Spring was a time for coughs and colds. None of this was unusual.

"No thank you," she said. "I'll be okay."

Cat's smile didn't reach his eyes as he pulled away from her, taking his drink with him. "The girl too polite to bother death, so she waits for it to come for her."

"I'm not dying, Cat."

"Ah, but you are," he said. "As you have tried before, but you might actually succeed this time. And the Caterpillar will be quite pleased when he learns. There was a time he wanted to send the other one after you. He will be pleased that he didn't need to waste his toy on such a rude child."

"What Caterpillar?" Lance asked, suddenly very alert.

"I'm going to get something to eat," Alice said. She had no appetite, but sitting here was worse than sitting in the cafeteria. She got to her feet, wavering the first steps before she found her footing and made her way for the door. Lance followed her out and they left Cat behind on the bed, watching them as he vanished from sight.

"Make no mistake," Cat said after her. "I take no pleasure in the truth. But you are not long for any world, Alice. And when you are ready, I will be as well."

CHAPTER 14

For Family

SHE WAS DOING this for Lance. If she didn't, he'd be trapped forever.

They caught a movie, which was a mercy. She kept her hands on her drink, and sat on his left where there was no hand for him to reach out to her. They didn't talk, though Arthur tried. Next to her, she could feel him growing annoyed that she wasn't responding, but he couldn't have suspected anything else. He threatened her to come out, after all, even if he didn't seem to realize it.

But when he managed to say something, Adrianna could feel that tug in her chest, that flutter building up inside. There were parts of her that wanted so badly for him to turn out to be secretly nice, that he needed to come out of that hard and terrible exterior. That she could find the good in him. And maybe if the circumstances had been different, she could have done that.

Trying to figure out what to do with your life when it was upended and everything was unfamiliar was no reason to threaten someone's family into a date. *Twice.* But after Lance was free, she would be free of her obligation and maybe she would never have to deal with him again. She knew Adam would help her with that if she needed help.

For right now, they stopped at Bakeology and took a seat in a booth. He paid for a slice of cake for each of them, Adrianna wondering idly where he was getting any of his money if he had no parents to provide him with it.

"You don't like me," he told her plainly.

Adrianna shifted uncomfortably across from him in the booth, not touching either her cake or the cup of coffee.

"It's okay," he said. "I understand. Lance has been trying to impart some of his wisdom. He was always much better with women than I was."

"Women?" Adrianna asked. "I'm only sixteen."

"With far more beauty than those years," Arthur told her. "You think I was holding your brother captive in order to make you come out with me today. I would have given him back to you whether or not you came, though. He's been very difficult lately."

Adrianna paid attention to that. "Difficult?" she asked,

leaning in. Difficult sounded dangerous for Lance. If Arthur didn't have control over the ghost, then she didn't know who did or what it would want. Lance might have been okay with him, but she didn't trust him.

"Usually he's much too loyal for his own good," Arthur said. "Wants the best for everyone around him to his own detriment. But he's found someone else to turn that attention onto lately, and he's been saying some things to me that I haven't heard in a very long time."

"Alice?"

Arthur nodded. "He wouldn't hurt her," he assured her. "But his tongue has gotten loose. He keeps saying that I need to leave this place and try to start my life again somewhere else. That being here is poisoning my chances of being happy." His eyes looked up at Adrianna and she found herself drawn in. "That pursuing someone so beautiful is clouding my judgment."

Adrianna resisted the urge to fall into those eyes. She tore her gaze away and took a sip of her coffee. "If I turn you down, you could leave," she told him. "There's nothing keeping you here."

It was Arthur's turn to look uncomfortable. He took a bite out of the chocolate cake in front of him and considered Adrianna. "If I'm being honest, your rejection wouldn't be enough to keep me away," he said.

"We call that stalking."

"Just being near you would be enough," Arthur said as if that was meant to reassure her. Warmth built up in her, followed by a distinct chill, but he wasn't done. "No, it wouldn't only be you. I would like very much to go back again."

Adrianna found that her cut into her cake was more of a stab. "Back?" She asked, already dreading the answer.

"Not just because she's there," Arthur assured her. "She needs to be stopped, make no mistake about that. The woman is insane. But there is something to it this time."

"To…" But Adrianna had lost the direction of this conversation. She didn't know who he was talking about and while she suspected the where, she couldn't be sure they were on the same page. "Back up. Where do you want to go back to? Who are you talking about?"

Arthur smiled, looking like he might reach across to touch her. He kept his hand to himself and on the fork. "Has Alice not mentioned Morgana? She's found her way out of the ice and into Wonderland." He frowned as she did, though for a much different reason. "Have you met her? She seemed to know Lance very well. Said he was her child for a while, but Mordred has been dead for a very long time."

Adrianna shook her head. "I don't know anyone named Morgana," she said. "I think there's a Morgan in one of Peter's classes, but that's about it."

"She looks a lot like you," he said. "Older. But you could have been sisters."

"What was she to you?"

"I believe the term you use would be my ex," he told her, shoveling another bite of cake into his mouth.

She'd heard the name before and finally placed it. Lance told her over the break he had a sister with that name. And now she learned that not only had he been seeing this sister, but that she looked like her. A few things fell into place and Adrianna's appetite vanished. "Oh."

Arthur didn't notice, already talking again around the cake in his mouth. "When I learned my wife was sharing my best friend's bed, I went to see her. Her son was already causing me problems with his uprising. I just wanted her to see *reason*. That she need not hoard Avalon, that I would only need its power for a short time. But ultimately she decided that was much too much and she tried to kill us all."

Adrianna would have liked very much to disappear. She didn't know how to react to anything he told her and so she stayed perfectly still as she listened. She didn't want her mind to make the connections it did, didn't want to know that she was now out with a boy her own age who had already once had a wife and another lover old enough to have a child that could be in an uprising, much less cause one. He looked young and acted it, but she was across from a very old man.

One that was interested in her in the same way he had once been interested in his sister. In a way he might still be interested in her.

And for a moment, he stopped. He stabbed at the cake again and ate more as if to soothe himself. When he let out a breath, his eyes drifted to the window, puzzlement across his features. "But there's something strange about those places. Neverland feels very much like it could have sprung from the womb of Avalon. Even Wonderland has an echo of it. Morgana may be insane, but there's a chance she's not wrong."

Adrianna couldn't stop thinking about how she reminded him of the sister he had probably had… She couldn't think about it any more than that. Even her irritation that everything in her life seemed to go right back to Wonderland was overshadowed by that and she wanted nothing more than to be done with this.

"Don't like it?" Arthur asked, reaching over and taking a bit of her cake off her plate. Adrianna pushed it across the table to him. "Your loss. It's really good."

"Are you really going to let Lance go?" Adrianna asked. For an old man that was creeping her out, he looked so young as he devoured the cake. Icing smudged his cheek when he looked up at her. "You're not going to just make that ghost friend of yours come back as soon as I tell you no the next time."

"You have my word," Arthur said. "Besides, I think I'm done with him. Bringing him back from an eternal slumber is enough penance for what he did to me."

"What did he do to you?"

"He slept with my wife."

Adrianna needed to stop asking questions. She knew that she wanted none of these answers, and she wasn't sure if it would be okay to leave. Worse, the thoughts of her brother being possessed by a much older man who was now going out with Alice made her worry that she had already let this go on for too long already. She felt helpless to stop any of it. She could only sit and wait for Arthur to finish his cake.

"How about we find Lance?" Arthur suggested with a smile. "I'll let him go right now."

Adrianna nodded dully and followed him out the door. At last, this was almost over.

THEY SPOTTED LANCE in the common area sitting near Sarah and Heather. They spread out several pages on the table, most of them marked with the bright colors Heather used to keep her life organized, chatting idly to one another. In the corner of the couch not paying any attention, Alice was curled up with a novel in her hands and looking like she might drift off to sleep at any moment.

Arthur stopped before they got close, eyeing Heather. "She doesn't like me much," he said, looking at Adrianna. "I can do it from back here, if you want to avoid the fight."

Adrianna nodded. She didn't mind so long as she had her brother back. The fewer steps and the less she had to ask of Arthur before he changed his mind, the better. As it was, the sooner she could stop having to deal with him the better. If he wanted to hide and do this, she didn't have the energy anymore to stop him out of fear she might learn still more that she didn't want to know about him.

Still, Adrianna felt weird watching her brother sitting there, too-confident grin plastered on his face as he spoke to Sarah. She wondered what would happen, if he would do something strange the moment that the ghost was gone. If this was the best time. He might collapse right there in the middle of the room or do something else embarrassing. This could be a bad idea.

Her misgivings piled up, but she couldn't stop Arthur now. His hand was already in sight as he stared at Lance and his fingers let out a dull snap. In front of her, Lance twitched, puzzlement across his face as his words stopped. He looked around, his eyes locking with Arthur's for only a moment before he went back to talking to Sarah, still the same person as he had been a moment ago. Still not Lance.

Arthur looked surprised by it. He snapped again, this time

his lips moving with the command. He changed the gesture, his brow furrowing, but still Lance did not return to himself. He let out a cough and once more shot a glare at Arthur, but that was all.

"It didn't work," Adrianna said, voice quiet. She had dealt with this day and the last, and still she didn't have her brother back. After all this, she didn't have him back. More than that, the one thing she thought was keeping the ghost in place wasn't.

Arthur couldn't get rid of him.

Beside her, Arthur tried to recover for himself. He waved it off, guiding her away from the common room. "He must know you're going to dump me as soon as he's gone," he said dismissively, but Adrianna wasn't fooled. She'd seen his shock that it didn't work. Seen that his attempts *wouldn't* work.

And if Arthur couldn't do it, then she would have to find another way. She'd come this far already. Alice was free of Wonderland, Adam was out of that horrible place. All that remained was Lance and, once that was done, they could go back to normal, she just had to figure out how to free Lance, and she had plenty of access to magic without having to rely on Arthur to do it for her.

She had one book under her mattress and somewhere in the room there were three more. She and Alice must have been missing something when they looked before. And now she had Arthur, who had summoned him in the first place. What he tried may not work now, but he knew something she didn't about how to deal with ghosts. Somehow, she would figure out how to free her brother. No matter what.

"Teach me," Adrianna told him. "I'll get rid of Lancelot myself."

CHAPTER 15

Bow Out

ALICE KEPT HER eyes on the book as she walked and flicked away the residue on her hand. She was coughing more now, her hand more often covered in phlegm by the time she could breathe again. Worse, where it had once been clear it was now coming away pinker and pinker as the days went on. If she just kept reading, she didn't need to think about it. Even if she had long ago run out of things in the library that interested her to read.

"You would rather die than be associated with us," Cat said, though he was strangely complacent in his words. It was more an observation than anything else. "The lengths of madness some will go to try and prove they are not mad. You are truly more like us than we could have ever imagined, even without your heart."

"Go away, Cat," she told him, starting to jog toward the

gym. She didn't make it far before she fell back into a walk, a pain building up in her chest again as she felt her lungs starting to protest already. Her legs hurt as she walked. All of her muscles hurt, but she knew she would notice it more today because she would have to use them more than in a typical gym class. She couldn't push herself too hard yet if she wanted to make it through club. "I can't go back."

"Oh, you can," he said. "You just can't use the mirrors anymore. Those were my way."

"I don't want to know mine," she said. "People like me now. I'm happy."

"Only the worst of people can find happiness without their heart, Alice," he said. "And no matter how you try, you cannot be the very worst of them. But if you are all right, I will not bring you back. I have been back. Ask and I will show you what you have allowed Wonderland to become. And make no mistake. You have allowed it to happen."

"You can't make me feel guilty," Alice told him. "I'm happy. I'm normal finally."

"Until you return to your father. Which you never will if you do not come back to Wonderland first. But don't think you're the only one that Wonderland has caught."

Alice tried to shoot a glare at Cat, but he was gone when she looked. She let out a sigh and she continued onward, feeling stronger and better as she continued moving. So long as she could keep going forward, so long as she could be normal, everything would be fine. And that was all she wanted to do. She brought her book back to her face and buried herself in it as she continued her slow walk to the gym.

She felt weak and dizzy by the time she got to the gym and was going to not make it much longer. The walk, it seemed, was too much for her. Later today would be some nice, relaxing studying and all she had to do was survive until she got to that. If club had to start at all.

Kevin was there with Heather and Adam standing around him, looking frantic. Alice joined them, catching bits of what was going on as she got closer. They hadn't noticed her just yet and she was starting to wonder if she was invisible, but it was soon very apparent that they were just very interested and concerned with what was happening with Kevin right now. And all the things he was saying. And why Kevin was here instead of Peter.

"I don't know where he went," Kevin said, looking like he was trying very hard to be calm about it but failing. He was thinking through his words before they came out, looking for the best way to say things and stopping himself before he went too far. "He just dis— He wasn't there this morning. And none of his friends know where he is. And his roommate, Kyle, he said he didn't hear him go anywhere. The window was open," he said, though it looked like he regretted it. "He just… I don't know. But the dorm advisors are looking for him. If any of you see him…"

"We'll keep an eye out," Heather assured him. "I'm sure he's just off for a run or something. It's almost midterms. He's probably just clearing his head. He'll turn up eventually. You sure he's not just sleeping in?"

"He wasn't there last night. I thought maybe he'd come back, but he never did."

"Have you reported it?"

"Yeah, everyone's looking now," he said. He looked up at Alice and started to rush towards her, catching himself before he got too far. "Hey, have you seen Peter?" he asked, looking around. "Or know where he might have gone? Did he say anything to you?"

Alice shook her head. "When did he leave?"

"Some time last night," he said, the eye contact much more meaningful than it needed to be. "He's been having trouble sleeping and waking up in weird places. Did he say anything about it to you?"

Alice shook her head, but she did remember what Peter had said. That he was just not sleeping so that he didn't wake up too far away. That he was worried that he was going to wake up in Neverland one day. Alice suspected today was that day, but she couldn't say that here with these people around.

Behind him, Adam looked like he knew what Alice did.

His eyes searched out Alice's, but she avoided them for now. He could seek her out later. Kevin was much more important right now.

"Sorry, he hasn't told me anything," Alice said. "I'll keep an eye out for him? But I'm sure the police will be better at tracking him down than anyone else."

Heather agreed and ushered Kevin off to the side, waving for the rest of them to get started with club activities. She sent them around for a jog to warm up and activities started, but Adam caught her by the arm before she could begin. She was almost glad for it, covering her mouth and starting to cough again. Adam waited for her to finish before dragging her over to begin with the wooden swords, something he was far better at than she was.

Alice didn't argue and let him lead her away, looking around to see that Lance was not there today to keep an eye on her. She would have to be a little extra careful today. After a drink from her water, she went to pull a chest guard off of the wall. Adam pulled her back from it, handing her a sword. "You don't need it," he said. "I won't if you won't."

"You won't anyway," Alice told him, taking it anyway and setting it in place, tapping the top of it to make sure it covered what she needed it to. She wasn't going to risk him doing anything that might show that there was a gaping hole in her chest. She wanted nothing more than to get this over with, feeling dizzy again and taking a seat on the ground. She waited for the feeling to pass before she looked back at him. "You're going to get hurt without one of these."

"Not from you," he said, an edge to his voice as he shoved the sword at her when she was done. "Come on, we need to talk. Try to keep up."

"You can't just grab coffee like a normal person?" Alice asked, already weary. Still, she felt better so long as she was moving, so she got to her feet and squared off, getting ready to deal with whatever Adam was angry about this time. She glanced back, seeing Kevin leaving with a final lingering look at Alice before she turned back on Adam.

It was just in time as Adam was already on her. She could tell that he pulled back, stopping before the first strike and falling into a different routine. Not a sparring match, but drills that Alice knew well enough that she could handle. She followed and fell into the pattern of it, stepping and moving her body as she needed to and letting her mind go free and wander as they moved. Or she had at first, until Adam decided he knew what he wanted to say to her.

"He's in Wonderland, isn't he?"

Alice was already getting winded, but she pushed through. "I don't know," she said.

"You *know* he's over there. So when are you going?"

"I'm not going."

"Don't be..." he started, then slowed in realization of what she just said. Alice kept going with the drills as best she could, and Adam tried to press her to go faster. Alice did not keep up and he relented, slowing down again. "Don't you lie, you know you're going over there as soon as you can. Midterms aren't stopping you. Nothing ever stopped you before."

"I can't go back anymore," Alice told him. Her lungs were on fire and she wanted to cough again. "I already told you. I'm done with Wonderland now. It's all over."

"Bullshit," Adam insisted. "You can't just—"

He drove harder, putting force behind his strikes, and Alice couldn't move fast enough. He smacked her hard in the shoulder and Alice fell backwards, landing hard on the ground in front of him. Her head spun as something bounced up into her throat. The cough she was trying so hard to suppress erupted from inside of her and racked through her, spreading up and throughout her body. She dropped the sword and covered her mouth as she hacked into her hands, feeling the phlegm landing in wet blobs in her palms.

She was dizzy and she picked a spot to stare at, waiting for everything around her to stop moving. What she found was Adam's knees and his voice continued over her, only a little concerned. "You okay?" he asked, less to make sure she was okay and more to ask if he could keep talking to her and have her actually listen.

"I'm okay," Alice said, looking in her hands. Red flecks looked back at her from her palms and she wiped it on her shirt, leaving behind a smear of pink. Adam didn't notice, his face souring at the sticky residue on her hands and pulled away his offer to help her up. "I'm not feeling well. Adrianna said I should probably take today off."

"Addie was probably right," Adam said, though it was clear he meant something else. He thought about it a moment before he reached down and pulled her up by her wrist, frowning as she rocked on her feet. "You look terrible, you know. If you just let me across, I can take care of it. I'll find him for you."

"I can't go across anymore," Alice told him again, still feeling faint and dizzy. She closed her eyes tight for a moment, wavering, and Adam ushered her to the side where she could sit down. "I can't open the mirrors. It's all over for me."

"That sounds like bullshit, Alice," he said.

"I don't know how else to tell you I can't do it anymore," she told him, looking up and trying to meet his eyes. She couldn't quite focus and he grabbed her a bottle of water to drink. "Thanks."

"How long?"

"When did Adrianna and Arthur start going out?"

"About the same time you and Lance did."

Alice nodded. "About that long," she said.

"Fine," he said in a way that told her it wasn't. "Go back. Get some rest. We'll talk again after I have a word with Lance."

"Or sometime tonight."

Adam glared at her, but he let it drop. "You can get back on your own?"

Alice nodded. "Give me a minute. I'll be okay."

She breathed deep and waited for the world to come back into focus around her. Her lungs were on fire. She didn't like any of this. Out of the corner of her eye, she saw a flash of purple in the window. Something was watching her and waiting for her to admit that he was right.

CHAPTER 16

Eavesdropping

ALICE WAS GONE when Adrianna woke up, already off at Combat Club. That suited Adrianna fine, more than happy to keep Alice from having to worry about any of this. She wondered if she would care that Lance would go back to the way he was. Surely she would like her actual brother more than this fake.

Not that Alice ever said what she liked about him. When they had a quiet moment, Alice never mentioned him. She didn't press, instead taking any of Alice's invitations to talk about Arthur and all the reasons he creeped her out now. Alice had provided an ear, but didn't understand why she would want to continue to talk to him.

Well, until she told Alice that he couldn't, in fact, get rid of the ghost.

Alice had been sympathetic, but ultimately she couldn't

help any more than she already had. She had already given Adrianna all of her notes and she could no longer grab the books herself. She couldn't so much as disappear anymore and her attempts at doing a spell were futile. Adrianna was on her own to figure this out. Mostly alone, anyway.

Adrianna pulled the white book out from under her mattress, but she couldn't find any answers there. There was something in there about sending various things to other places, but she didn't know how to conceptualize a ghost that was so deeply entwined into her brother. She didn't know how to get rid of one without accidentally sending the other away. It was a start, but it wasn't the solution. Not until she had a better understanding.

And unfortunately, that better understanding would have to come from Arthur.

She took a photo of the pages of the white book she wanted to use and hid it away again. Carefully, she put the sheets and blankets over everything, glancing back at Alice's unmade bed and wondering if this was a good idea. Alice knew things about these books and about how they worked. The spells came easier to her. She would know how to do this and Adrianna wouldn't have to talk to Arthur at all.

But Alice had been so much better. Despite her questionable taste in a facsimile version of her brother, she'd seen Alice come out of her shell. She was talking to people, offering answers in class, and not vanishing on the weekends without a word. She might be getting sick given how bad that cough was getting, but she was also so much calmer. She was living a life here that she could maintain, without the constant stress of Wonderland.

Adrianna couldn't drag her back into this. It was her brother and she could figure out how to get him back. And when he was, they could all be free of that cloud that this had brought on all of them.

She went out into the hall and headed for the stairs. Lance lived a floor up from them and Arthur shared his room. Arthur hadn't thought to ask for her number, so she didn't have it to make sure he was there that morning. It occurred to her that he might be at Combat Club with Alice this morning, but she was already on the way to the stairs when the thought hit her. At this point, there was no harm in seeing if he missed it for the day.

At the stairs, she spotted Sarah and Wyatt chatting, leaning in close and smiling as they exchanged quiet words. When Wyatt spotted her, he didn't separate from Sarah, waving her over and smiling as she joined them. "Hey," he said.

"Addie!" Sarah said brightly. "We're heading to Book Club. You're still invited."

Wyatt looked shocked next to her, tugging lightly at her arm and tilting his head, a concerned noise escaping his lips.

Sarah laughed and pat him gently on the arm. "Addie knows about so much more of it. Trust me, she probably needs it too."

Adrianna was about to protest, not interested at all in a book club, until she remembered what Sarah was talking about. Book club was what she had called the meeting of all the people who had been taken by the Bandersnatch before. She couldn't remember being invited herself, only that Sarah had asked her to extend the invite to Alice.

"I'm okay," she said. She wasn't sure what she could contribute. She had never met the Bandersnatch. The closest she had come was the Jubjub birds that had once guarded it, and she didn't want to impede what was happening there. "I actually need to..." she pointed up the stairs, not wanting to say just who she would see.

Neither Sarah nor Wyatt questioned it. "Sure," Sarah said. "Invite's open if you ever change your mind, though."

Adrianna went around them and up the stairs, almost wishing they had asked her to stay longer. If they had asked again, she might have joined them and abandoned all of this. He might not even be in the room to begin with, and she would have the chance to go back and join them anyway. At the very least, she could walk awkwardly past them again and see if she could come up with a reason it would be okay to join them.

She made it up to the right floor and her pace slowed as she turned the first corner. There were people milling about, watching her as she went past. The boys' side of the dorms were not usually privy to many girls and she felt very watched as she walked down the hall.

Any hopes that Arthur was at Combat Club melted away as Adrianna got closer to Lance's room. She could hear his muffled voice yelling from several doors down. Adrianna's heart clenched, knowing it was much too late now. She was already here and so was he. And she had something specific to ask.

Gripping her phone, she crept closer to the door. She just had to ask how to make this spell work and if it would work at all. One answer and she could leave. She didn't need to be here long, didn't have to tolerate him for long. She could do this.

"You don't even *want* to be here!" she heard Arthur roar from the other side of the door. Adrianna stopped in the hall at the sound, staring at the door and easing toward it to better hear what was happening inside. Someone came out of the room next to them, smacking their door hard as they left in, yelling at them to shut up.

Inside, Arthur didn't seem to care as he continued. "I told her I would send you away! *You* complained about being brought back from the dead! What is the problem? You're free! I absolve you of all your obligations to me! You've repaid me for your infidelity. Go!"

There was silence after that and Adrianna eased herself even closer to the door to try to hear what was being said.

"You aren't even going to say anything?"

"You're not done yet," came Lance's voice.

"*The whole point is I'm done with you!*" Arthur yelled back at him. "And now you've made me a liar! Even in death, you're still causing me problems. What, are you going to sleep with her too? Or are you too busy with the crazy one? Telling *me* I'm out of line for pursuing someone my age and there you are with a young girl of your own!"

"She *is* too young," Lance said. "And she is not Morgana, no matter how you might want her to be."

Adrianna felt that impulse to leave again. She didn't like hearing other people talk about her this way, though she couldn't quite figure out why. It made her uncomfortable, like her insides were all trying to escape her skin at once and run.

"I know that! Why would I want her to be, anyway?" Arthur demanded. "She tried to kill me. Her son tried to kill me! I don't want another woman like that in my life. Or one that would think it's fine to find comfort with you just because I'm not there."

Silence fell over the room. Adrianna strained to hear

something on the other side of the door, pressing her ear into the crack, but there was nothing there. For a long moment, Adrianna waited to hear anything, watching the other doors in the hall for someone else to come out.

"Now you're done," Lance said, his voice far too calm. "I will leave on my own in my due time. You kept me here long enough to earn a debt to repay."

"A debt?" Arthur demanded. His voice was quieter than before, but no less irritated. "To who? Not to me. I've already released you of everything."

"One debt to repay and I will be gone," Lance said. "And don't you worry, that debt will be done soon enough."

"This has to do with that girl, doesn't it? She knows you're keeping her real friend locked away, doesn't she?"

"You should be turning your attention to Morgana. The real one. You know what she's trying to do. She's already halfway there and you can't rely on Alice to stop her any longer. You need to find whoever's holding Neverland and keep them safe so she can't get her hands on them."

"Why would I care about what Morgana does? So long as I'm here, she won't touch me. She can do whatever she wants to Wonderland and Neverland. Try to remake them into Avalon if she thinks she can. It doesn't matter while I'm here. I won't be brought back."

"But you think if she gets Avalon back, she'll come for you next."

Arthur paused. "And you think she won't."

"I think if she gets Avalon back, she'll kill many people. And that's just as bad. There was a time you would have cared about that too."

There was silence followed by a shuffling. "Look," Lance said. "Find out who watches over Neverland and make sure Morgana doesn't find them."

"And you expect me to believe you're fraternizing with that girl just to watch over Wonderland, is that it?" Arthur demanded.

"Yes," Lance said, his voice distinctly closer.

If they said anything else, Adrianna didn't hear it. She dashed away and back down the stairs, her mind spinning and trying to put together what she heard. So many things were said and Adrianna didn't know what to make of them, from Arthur furious that the ghost refused to obey them to word that Morgana was trying to bring back Avalon using Wonderland and Neverland. She didn't understand half of what had happened, but one thing stuck out in her mind.

Lancelot said he would leave as soon as the debt was repaid, whatever that was, and it would be soon. Maybe all she had to do was wait.

CHAPTER 17

Study Time

LANCE FOUND HER as she made her way back to the dorm and Alice was grateful for that. She was drenched in sweat and she could almost feel the hole in her chest showing through as she wavered and stumbled no matter how she tried to walk normally. Lance slipped in next to her and let her lean on him as they walked.

"You aren't going to last much longer, Alice," he told her gently as he walked with her back to the dorms. "You're dying. You have to know that."

"It's fine," Alice said. He was nice and solid and made it so much easier to walk.

"It's not," Lance insisted, putting an arm around her as they walked. She certainly felt more stable, and warmer. She hadn't realized how cold she was despite the sun beating down and the sweat running down her face.

"And it's fine that you've kept Lance locked away this long?" she asked.

He stiffened up next to her and she lurched to the side before he caught both of them. He stopped looking at her, she could tell, and kept walking them back to the dorms. "I'm still here, you know," Lance said, and this time it was really him. His strides got shorter and he felt more stiff as they walked. "And I'm *pissed* you're only letting me out because she's going to fall if I run."

"I haven't seen you in ages."

"I've seen you. You want him to keep me quiet so no one tells anyone you're dying."

"I'm just coming down with something," Alice said. "I'm sorry."

"That's not going to work, Alice," Lance said bitterly. "You're keeping me locked up as much as he is. And for what? Is this really worth it?"

"Yes," Alice said. She coughed, stopping them as her body started shaking. Lance grabbed her as she doubled over, helping keep her upright as the coughs rocked through her. "I'm sure he'd let you out more if you just promise not to say anything. Besides, everyone likes me better this way. Heather's talking to me again. Adrianna doesn't look so worried when she looks at me anymore. It's all better now."

"It's not worth it," Lance said, his body shifting again as

they made it to the dorms. Lance was gone, the ghost taking his body over again as he led her to the elevator. "I'll say it again, Alice. You are dying."

"I can't go back, even if I wanted to," Alice reminded him as they made it to the room at the end of the hall. Though he was already helping her open the door, her mouth kept moving and words continued to spill out. "The mirrors don't work anymore. And besides, I can't be dying. If I was, it would have happened already, like when Lance had his removed, right? I've gone this long without my heart. I'm probably just sick with something. Besides, I've already almost died before. And then it didn't happen. It won't happen again."

"Maybe get some rest," Lance suggested as he left her at the door. "And skip studying tonight."

Alice let him go and made her way to the bathroom, grabbing her clothes on the way. She wasn't so much tired as she was completely exhausted and not sure she wanted to stand for so long. She turned the taps on and let the tub start to fill, crawling in and lying back against the edge of the tub before the water was high enough to even cover her feet.

For all Lance kept insisting she was dying, she knew it probably wasn't true. If she was, she would have died when her heart came out in the first place, like Lance had. She wasn't possessed by a ghost keeping her alive, so she was probably more like the people in Wonderland than she thought.

It made sense, given how the madness had been seeping in so strongly before and it was gone now along with her heart.

Her fingers drifted to the hole. Water never went into it when she showered somehow, yet she could stick her whole hand inside if she wanted. There was no point in arguing with either of them. Cat was convinced too, and would appear to tell her again soon enough. But with how the weather was changing, she was likely just getting sick. It had been a long time since she even had a cold. This was probably just the early signs of a flu and nothing she needed to be concerned about.

Alice relaxed in the hot water, watching it steam around her and idly rubbing at her fingers as she regained her strength. Yes, only a flu. It would explain why she was so tired and the cough. Why her body ached and why she was starting to feel so dizzy. Why she felt cold even as the weather was warming up.

And even if she was dying…

She got out of the shower and dressed, carefully adjusting the sports bra to cover the hole. Looking at it again, she could swear that the hole was getting bigger and the collar of the bra was only barely covering it now. Or maybe she was just wearing it so much now that it was stretching out. Still, she didn't want to alarm anyone with a strange shadow.

Loose clothes. She was already cold, so she threw on layers and tried to do what she could to make herself warmer.

It seemed to cover whatever it was that was happening in her chest and she went to the mirror. If she looked pale and unwell, then she could fix that too. She might not be as good as Sarah, but she knew how to do the basics and made herself up enough to make it look like she was fine.

She felt better when she was done and looked more normal. She grabbed her bag, one that was feeling heavier and heavier as the days passed, and made her way down to a small theater they commandeered as their study room for the evening. A movie played quietly in the background, but no one was paying any attention to it. Already Sarah and Robert were working through their homework and trying to help one another with what was going on. Adrianna had also taken refuge in there and was half way through a page of History when she looked up.

"Hey," Alice said, putting her stuff down. "No Kevin?"

Sarah looked up at her and then looked again, peering closer at her a second time. She frowned at the look of Alice and Alice knew immediately that she could tell she was wearing something on her face. Still, she made no comment and Alice wasn't about to bring it up.

"He's coming," Robert said, looking back at his phone. "He's been trying to figure out Peter all day. Can you believe he just vanished like that?"

"Yeah," Sarah said. "I'm more surprised that Alice hasn't

been this year. Guess all you needed was someone to stick around for." She smiled back at her, though there was something else in the look. "He's invited if you want."

"I..." Alice looked at her, then back to Adrianna. Adrianna avoided her eyes and Alice wasn't really sure what was going on. She still didn't know what to do with the repeated accusations that she and Lance were going out, but she was certain fighting it wasn't worth the effort. "Okay," she said.

She settled in and started working, happy that there was no follow up. She didn't really need the time to look at the material again, already knowing most of this from her time with Ms. Miller and still remembering most of it from her classes. When she was done, she picked up a book out of her bag and started to read.

Kevin tried to focus on homework and studying when he joined them, but he was clearly still distracted by Peter's disappearance. His eyes kept wandering, first to the phone next to him, then to Alice with that look like he desperately wanted a word with her. She couldn't do anything to help him, so she avoided his eyes.

Adam and Heather came in together later and had a quiet word with Kevin. They did their best to assure him that it was going to be alright. There was a pang of guilt, especially when Adam tried to drift closer to her, but Heather kept him away for the moment. Alice was grateful for her actions and her telling looks that Adam couldn't see to tell Alice that she was not happy with him right now.

That look soon changed to interest when a new face appeared in the door. Lance leaned in, nodding for Alice to come join him outside. Again, Heather tugged at Adam's hand, pulling him further into the room and getting out of the way as Alice went out to meet him.

Lance wasn't alone in the hall, Arthur grabbing her as soon as she was out and yanking her away from the door and the frosted glass wall where they might be seen. He kept pulling her until they were well away, down the hall and tucked into a different theater entirely. "Peter's missing," he said. "Really missing."

"I'm aware," Alice said, not trying to fight her way out of his grip. Lance gently pried him off of her and she sagged against the cool glass while the dizziness of the actions passed. "So? You don't care about Peter."

"I care that he's missing," Arthur said. "You and him. If you both go missing, that means Morgana's going to try to do something. And she cannot be allowed to get Avalon back. She's going to try to lure you to her and use you to dismantle Wonderland. And you like that god-forsaken cesspool of a world. What are you going to do to stop that?"

"I'm not going back to Wonderland."

"You don't have a choice. She's going to make you."

"He's going to turn you into a rabbit and keep you in our room," Lance said.

"Oh, like hell you are," came Adam, bursting in and trying to step between them. Alice thought he was trying to be protective for only a moment, but that wasn't the case at all. He wanted his chance at her, rounding on her and looking like he might assault her next while Lance tried to pull him back. Alice fought the urge to check and make sure her shirts were in place and covering, but she knew they were. It was fine. "Better idea. You take us across and we deal with this now. Clearly there's something else that happened."

"Morgana happened," Arthur informed him. "The Queen is gone, long live the Queen. Your sister made way for her to come into power and now she's going to dismantle both of the worlds, destroy them like she did Avalon."

"Who the hell is Morgana?"

"There's no problem," Alice told them both. "I can't get back to Wonderland anyway. So there's nothing to be worried about."

"Bullshit," Adam snapped as he turned back around to look at her.

"It seems they don't believe you either, Alice dear."

He appeared around her shoulders as a large purple cat, the weight of him almost too much for how weak she felt. She leaned back against the wall, but his claws dug into her shoulders and she couldn't feel his weight at all anymore. "Go away, Cat."

"So mad that you can't use my door anymore," he said. "But the mirrors were never the gateway for you. You just stole them from me. A taste of a middle wish pie, stolen from the king and his cat in one fell swoop. But just because you don't have the mirrors doesn't mean that you can't be there anymore. You have your own way across."

"What on earth is that?" Arthur demanded.

"Cat!" Adam exclaimed.

"Hello again," Lance said with a frown.

"So you *can* get back across," Adam said, glaring back at her.

"I can't," Alice told him firmly. "If you missed it in his monologue, I can't use the mirrors anymore. I don't know any other way to get across."

"Rabbit hole?" Adam suggested.

"I don't know how to find those. I'm trapped here. And that means Morgana can't get to me here either. So it's all good. I'm sorry about Peter, I really am, but I can't do anything about that." Her head was spinning and vision blurred, but Cat kept her on her feet. "I don't know what will convince you."

"With him here, we won't need you," he said, his attention turning to Cat. "You can take me back there, can't you?"

The Cheshire Cat grinned wide. "He thinks I will listen to his demands," he said.

Adam made a grab for the Cheshire Cat, but he vanished away from her shoulders. She sagged against the glass again, but her head was mostly clear now as Cat drew their attention into the corner. He winked at her as Adam made another grab for him, Lance gently explaining to Arthur that the Cheshire Cat could get to Wonderland if necessary.

Seeing her chance, she left the room. The tickle in the back of her throat soon stopped her, turning into another coughing fit, and she leaned against the wall to keep from tumbling to the ground. Maybe she should head back to her room and get some rest. This flu did seem to be getting much worse and a nap would do her some good.

"What they've forgotten," Cat said, only his smile appearing next to her, "is that no matter what changes, Alice will always be Alice will always be Alice."

CHAPTER 18

Cover Blown

GYM WAS ALMOST a break from the tests that dominated this week. Adrianna was stressed and being told that all she had to do to pass this class was to run two miles in half an hour was a nice change of pace from the worry and the constant studying. And she needed to study. She could process information better now, but she needed to get that information into her head. Word by word, she processed and synthesized her work. Her grades were better, almost as good as Alice's or Heather's now, but she felt like she needed to work a lot harder than either of them to get there.

Worse, she was also spending more and more of her spare moments poring through the pages of the white book and looking through Alice's notes on the others. She practiced the spells where she could, trying to figure out a way to free her brother without having to talk to Arthur. She met him once to get him to teach her how to focus on the right part of Lance to send the spirit away, but he had treated her like she didn't know what she was doing and continued to try to touch her, to position her hand or her head or move her hair.

It wasn't worth it, so she had started a new tactic. When she was alone, she would perform a little more and a little more until she got stronger, sharper, more precise. It was too slow, but she was seeing improvement. If the ghost was not out of her brother soon, she could do it herself. Once midterms were done, she could work on it more.

And so she jogged. She was never that fast, falling well short of Sarah who liked the exercise, but today she had Alice join her. Heather and Sarah even hung back, keeping the slow pace and taking advantage of the downtime of the class to try to catch up before they had split up in the evening for their clubs and more studying.

"So, we need to celebrate after we're done with this week," Heather said. "Girls only, though."

"No arguments," Adrianna said. "Movies?"

"Movies *in town*," Sarah suggested. "Let's get off campus and have a little fun. It's not like we're going to be missing anyone for the weekend, right?" She looked pointedly back at Alice, who was starting to trail behind them. "Are you doing okay?"

If she was being honest, Alice was doing terribly lately. Adrianna had passed it off as exam stress. Between one brother being possessed and another one still looking like he needed to get back into a mirror, not to mention dealing with Arthur insisting he could teach her better than she could teach herself, she had let Alice tell her she was just fine and nothing to worry about. But she was definitely sick, though she refused to see the nurse to get a pass to excuse herself from gym or anything else for the week. She was coughing a lot lately and having trouble concentrating. She always seemed to be cold, even when the weather was warming up. She was even wearing a sweatshirt today, and she was sweating bullets as they went for a light run. This was usually easy for her, and she looked like she was struggling. Adrianna hadn't noticed how much makeup Alice was wearing to make herself look normal, but with it now running off her face it was hard to miss how ill she was.

"I'm coming down with something," Alice said.

"You've been coming down with something for weeks," Heather said. "I think it's time for you to stop at the nurse. Like, now."

Alice coughed, as she was doing more and more often now, shaking her head. "I'll be fine," she said between hacking coughs that brought her to a halt. The rest of them stopped too, hovering around her and ready to give her a hand. She tipped over and let out a nervous laugh, grabbing Heather who kept her upright and she shakily stood back up. Heather held her arm and looked concerned.

"You're shaking," Heather said.

"I'm okay," Alice insisted, pulling herself away and taking a few tentative steps. "Come on," she said, heading up in front of them and starting to jog again. None of them followed her, watching Heather for guidance, not that she knew what she was supposed to do either. Not until Alice pitched forward.

Heather lurched for her and grabbed Alice by the wrist as she fell down to the dirt. She broke her fall, but Alice was clearly out cold. Heather lowered her slowly to the ground, making sure she didn't hit her head in the fall. Sarah and Adrianna crowded in on her and Heather frowned at her hand. "Gross," she said, looking at whatever had been there for only and instant before wiping it on her shorts. She thought about it for a moment and then crouched down next to Alice, getting Sarah out of the way as she grabbed her hand to look at it.

She turned Alice's hand over to show the splash of red in her palm. Wide eyed, Heather turned back to Sarah and snapped, "Go get Ms. Hyuna, now. Addie, what's going on? How long has she been sick?" She resettled Alice properly on her back and put her ear by Alice's mouth. She waited a moment before a small look of relief washed over her and she looked down to press her fingers into Alice's neck, first one spot. Then another. Then another.

"I don't— She said she was fine!" Adrianna said, looking down at her. Alice was sweating and breathing at least, but there was something strange in the way her chest rose and fell.

"Yeah, well, she lied," Heather said, the frown on her face deepening as she kept moving her fingers around Alice's neck, her fingers searching for a vein that would give her some hint of what was going on. "It's Alice. Don't tell me you're that surprised."

"What's wrong?" Adrianna asked, watching as Heather let out a low grunt and pulled her hand back.

"It's fine, I just can't seem to find her pulse," she said. "She's breathing. That's the important thing. When she gets up, we'll get her back and we'll force her to go to the nurse. She's been eating, right? And keeping it down?"

"Not as much as usual," Adrianna noticed, but her eyes went elsewhere. If Heather couldn't find a pulse, then the way her sweater was pooling in the middle of her chest was suddenly very suspicious. "You've been there."

"Do you know if she's been doing anything else we should know about?" Heather asked, her voice dropping and looking up and down the trail. "It's like she's been a completely different person since she started seeing Lance. Do you know if they've been—"

"No," Adrianna said firmly. Lance would never. *Alice* would never. "There's no drugs or anything like that."

"You can't be sure, Addie. Alice is really good at keeping..."

Heather put her hand on Alice's chest and Adrianna watched as her hand pressed down much too far into her chest. Heather's eyes went wide and pulled back. She stared down at Alice like she was something not human. "Oh, that's weird," she said breathlessly. There was a beat before Heather tried again, pressing just a little further than before. Nothing stopped her hand. It definitely passed into where Alice's ribs should have stopped her. "Oh..."

Adrianna's eyes were wide as it all clicked together what was going on. A series of plans happened in her head all at once and she saw Alice's eyes starting to move under her eyelids. She was coming around and she knew for certain she did not want Heather around to hear what she had to say.

Adrianna's mouth moved words sharp and precise, her fingers twitching in front of her. She needed Heather to do precisely what she said. Believe what she said. Heather's eyes went glassy in front of her as Adrianna finished, the spell. "Nothing weird happened," she told Heather, more a command than anything else. "Alice is waking up. I'll bring her. You let Ms. Hyuna know we're coming."

Heather got up and left obediently. Adrianna waited for her to jog out of sight before she moved. A very small part of her was amazed it worked, but it was very quickly squashed by the feelings building up inside her as she saw Alice stir next to her. Ones she didn't know how to put in order, and ones that were ready to burst, fueled by betrayal and stress.

Alice had a hole in her chest where her heart should be. She had seen it once before, had seen her brother die in front of her without his heart. And it was happening again.

"*How long?*" Adrianna demanded as Alice opened her eyes. She was still on her feet and she was furious as Alice came back around. Alice stayed on the ground, staring back at her with bleary eyes and trying to focus. It didn't matter that she was barely moving, Adrianna's mind racing and going through how scared she was in that moment with Lance. Knowing that Alice was doing the same. "What happened and *how long have you been keeping this from me?*"

"Keeping what?" Alice asked. Her words slurred and she rolled her head back against the ground. Her eyes pressed shut and she tried to roll onto her side, struggling with even that and letting herself flop back onto her back.

Adrianna didn't care. She hadn't raised her voice to anyone in a long time, but now she was letting loose. She bent forward, jabbing her finger directly into the sweatshirt and letting it go in where it shouldn't be. The action made a chill run through her. *"You lost your heart! When, Alice?"*

"I..." She looked down at the finger sticking into her chest and tried to back away. Adrianna let her, let her think and let her respond. But she was quiet and thinking.

"When?" Adrianna asked. It was now that she realized the tears stinging her eyes, that she was mad and crying all at once and furious that this was happening. "How long has it been gone?"

"A while," Alice said. She sat herself up on the ground, but didn't try to get to her feet, her head sinking into her hand as she took in slow, even breaths. "I'm—"

"I swear to god if you try to say you're fine or you're okay..."

Alice stopped talking at least. She sagged in her spot and took in another breath before looking back up at her. "I'm sorry."

"Wonderland isn't better, is it?" she asked.

"I don't know," she said. "I really can't go back. Not since I lost my heart, I can't go back. I can't do anything anymore. I'm just normal."

"Alice, you can't live without a heart!" Adrianna wasn't sure what she could say to make her understand. She was too calm about this. Too okay with what had happened to her. Just like always. "Why wouldn't you just tell me?"

Alice struggled to put her words together and come up with the right thing to say. Adrianna was crying and she knew it, but she wouldn't stop just because it was happening. Alice had kept this from her, had probably purposefully kept it from her. She was mad at Alice for not saying anything and mad at herself for not realizing there was something wrong. She had been so different. She should have known that something was wrong. She should have seen it coming.

"Is it time the liar tells the truth?" A purple head came out from around Alice's side, the cat so large that he came up to Alice's shoulder. Or maybe, she had shrunk. "Such a pretty lie, but it is all coming apart. Because you have never been that good of a liar. An honest girl forced to lie is a terrible liar to us. Only someone who would want the lie would believe you."

"Go away, Cat."

"Such a pretty lie," he continued, his eyes glinting as he looked for just a moment at Adrianna, just enough to let her know that this was for her more than for Alice. "Wonderland left you alone. You could be normal at last. Everyone likes you more, talks to you more, listens to you more. And all you had to do was look the other way while she tried to take apart Wonderland. And we allowed it for a time. We hoped that we did not need to implement Plan C. But now, we must. It is the way you've chosen."

"There was a plan A?" Adrianna asked through tears. How had she missed all of this?

"Of course not. There was a first plan and it was terrible. You cannot keep Alice out of Wonderland no more than you can trust Alice to not do precisely what she should not. There were several not-plans. Tiger Lily decided that we would try to take the heart back from the witch. The Mad Hatter said many things about keeping the witch from getting her hands on the boy from Neverland and did none of them."

"And plan C?"

"Plan Caterpillar," he said. "Make the heart useless."

"And how do you do that?"

"Alice dies," Cat said, rubbing quietly up against Alice. "And then Wonderland finds someone else. And no one goes to fetch them."

Adrianna felt that pang of betrayal, of doom and of sadness. Of determination to fight and hopelessness that it was too late. She didn't know how to process what was going on. And, more frustratingly, Alice was adjusting in her usual way.

"So why do you keep telling me I can come back whenever I want?" Alice asked. She was too calm about the whole matter, too accepting. Too tired and not angry. She had seen it before only a year ago, back when she would be killed by the Bandersnatch. She was far too okay with everything that happened to her, too accepting that it would happen whether or not she wanted it to. She didn't fight and Adrianna couldn't understand why. Alice could do so many things. She found solutions for the other problems in her life and worked so hard. And when it came to herself, Alice was so willing to just accept whatever was handed to her.

But Adrianna wouldn't let it happen. She would stop it from happening however she had to. She had learned magic and she would find a way to go there. She had gotten rid of the Queen of Hearts, so she could do this. Morgana would not stop her. She would put an end to her.

"Because why would anyone want to die here?" he asked. "Especially you. You have gotten so close already. You will remember." He rubbed up against her again. "We like you Alice. You're mad. We're mad. I would like one last tea. I hope we will have it before you go."

CHAPTER 19

Echoes of Avalon

THE ISLAND WAS a peaceful and serene place. This they knew. A place of magic where all your needs would be met. It invited children and fulfilled the dreams the world would never grant them. The world was a cold place for many and the island would allow them to grow in a place where they could find safety. If safety was what they wanted.

There were five young girls who made the island home who knew more than they should of the world. Or one did. She had grown curious and left the island once to see how the world had changed and to experience the outside. While she was away, she learned many things, but ultimately decided her life should be on the island with her sisters. But now, the outside world returned to her.

A man appeared with his mentor. Arthur and Merlin.

Men she had loved before and still loved, even now. It didn't matter that one was in part her brother, her blood, her family. It did not matter that the other was so old that he was time-less, but chose to age with every passing year. Perhaps not every passing year. Morgana had chosen to stop experiencing time as well once she came back to the island. That was the mercy of the island.

She met them on the beach and did not realize what they were here for. Not at first. But it soon became clear. He came to tell her about the things that had happened on the main-land, to tell her of his trouble, and for a night of comfort. She would listen to him with open arms and an open heart because she missed him so and she wanted to know every-thing that she left behind on the mainland and that world of men.

Her son had started a bid to take the crown by force. He was not entitled to it, but it was what he wanted. Her brother had come home to find his loving wife in bed with the man he trusted most. She didn't see what was so bad about it. She had been with this other man herself in her life, and she did not see a need to keep love so private and selfishly to yourself. But Arthur did, and he was vengeful when he wanted to be. And right now he wanted to be.

But Merlin had weaseled his way into his ear. Promised him that magic would resolve all of his problems. That they must take the magic from the island. She wanted to help him however she could, but the magic of the island was not hers to give. She would share it freely with any that were deemed worthy by the island, but the island would decide what it wanted to give. She would let him in, would care for him, would help him any other way. But Avalon would decide who was to use its power.

Avalon did not favor her as it once had. Morgana had been all right with that. As she stayed, she grew more youthful and returned slowly to her place. With her sisters. To the island. But she would never be in the same favor as she once was. She needed to find another way to help. And she would.

But then there was the play that Merlin made, that Arthur followed. They would find a way. The old man tried to seize the power while Arthur and his sorrows and his touch distracted her. And she was distracted. So distracted. And it was too late.

Her sisters had run and hidden, but Morgana would not hide from them. She had known them and she knew that this was the will of men. That this was what happened when you let them have their revenge too often. She had been one of them, and it would happen no longer. Merlin would not drain her home of all it was so he could gain power. So he could help Arthur enact a revenge on his wife who had been lonely. On her son who had not learned restraint on his impulses and his pride. On his friend who had found himself only wanting to provide comfort.

Oh, Lancelot. She might miss him most of all.

If the island was to be protected, then none could have it at all. And so she plunged it into ice, preserving it and all that were inside for all eternity. They wouldn't die, but they would be trapped there forever until such a time that the island decided that they had learned their lesson.

And the world around them changed. Avalon and Arthur's kingdom passed from the memory, but the island was not done. It did not want to be sitting alone forever encased in ice. And so the island began to melt away, keeping its people trapped and frozen and finding new innocents to bring to it. It had brought the five sisters once, and it brought more now. The island remained, but the magic drained away into two new lands, ones that children could take over and shape them.

One land was created by a boy. He had been so lonely and so he had been given a place to stay, to grow, and for his imagination to flourish. He never grew up because he had never wanted to. He stayed and the magic was simply a part of his life, not one that he would use. And the island liked this very much.

The other was a stranger place, one made by fancies and only visited. It had liked that Morgana brought back new things, and so this other island was made, one that would be filled with wonder for children to pass into and out of as they needed it, to shelter them when they needed. And gradually, some of the children decided to stay.

ALICE STIRRED IN her bed but she didn't want to open her eyes. If she woke up, she might actually have to figure out what she was supposed to do next to make them happy. Because Adrianna was very unhappy with her now.

She'd done everything she should. Made them happy. She stopped going to Wonderland, stopped being distracted by it. Her father would be pleased to hear her not talking so strangely any longer. Her grades were improving and she was a normal student at last. Heather was talking to her again. Adrianna didn't look so worried when she looked at her.

Her heart for normalcy was a fine price for her, but not anyone else.

Finally, she let her eyes creak open to find she was alone in the room. She was safe, but she had no desire to think about this any longer. She wasn't even sad about any of it, just tired. There was no way for anyone to be happy. And the more she thought about it, the more tired she got. She needed a distraction.

Alice reached over the side of her bed, pulling a book off the pile and opening it. Pushing herself up so that her back was pressed against the wall, feet curled up under her, she stared at the page and was already bored. Another book she had read before. She was bored with it and already her mind was wandering as she tried to make herself process each of the words.

Cat kept insisting that she could go back whenever she wanted, but Wonderland remained elusive to her. The only place for her to escape was into the worlds of these books, ones with problems that could be resolved more simply, with killing the right person or finding true love to support you. But Alice didn't want to kill anyone, and she doubted someone without a heart could ever fall in love. Wonderland had never asked that of her. It had never been clear what it was asking, but it was never that.

Maybe she really was dying. And if she was, she really would have liked that one last tea.

When she looked up from the pages, she saw a tea party set out and waiting for her. A place with friends around the table. Or it was a single tea set in a garden, a place where she could be alone. It was like the place on the top of the school building, where she could be alone and surrounded by something familiar. And so she went to it, leaving her book behind on the bed.

CHAPTER 20

Game Plan

ADRIANNA LET ALICE sleep and worked furiously on her phone, trying to put together something else that she could do. And she knew she had to do *something*. They had gotten Lance's heart back, so she knew it was possible to put a heart back once it had been removed.

For Alice to put it back. Adrianna had never done it herself. And the thought of doing it...

She tried not to think about that. They just needed to get her heart back so she wouldn't die. The Caterpillar was heartless and she wouldn't stand for the plan. Wonderland was not worth Alice's life.

Alice had been fine. But she really hadn't been. Her health had fallen apart, but being away from Wonderland had been so good for her otherwise. She was focusing on school. She was closer to her friends now than she'd possibly ever been. She was better without it. She'd even gotten into a relationship, however strange that was. She was finally living normally. Everything was better without Wonderland except for the fact that Alice was dying, but she could at least adjust to not having it in her life anymore. They were at least on the right track. She was developing a future.

But that future meant nothing if she wasn't alive to see it. It pained Adrianna to know that Alice had been slowly getting worse and she hadn't noticed with all the other things happening in her own life. With dealing with Arthur and being wrapped up in the magic she was learning. In her brother being possessed and her other brother still so determined to get back to Wonderland. At least Heather was keeping him here and focused, but Adrianna wasn't sure how well or how long that would last.

Wonderland needed to go. But first, they had to get the heart back so Alice could live. There had to be another way. She knew there was another way.

As soon as Alice was in bed and asleep, Adrianna went into action. It didn't matter that it was the middle of the week or that they still had classes and midterms to deal with. They needed to figure out how to save her, and that involved working with people who didn't feel the need to like her while she was at it. She called Arthur first, asking him to the movie room, and both of her brothers. Lance came with Arthur and Adam lingered far from both of them, clearly not liking that Arthur was here at all. Especially given the company he brought.

"Whatever this is, you don't need them," Adam told her sharply. "Where's Alice?"

"Sleeping," Adrianna snapped back at him.

It was so sharp that it took him aback. His eyes went automatically back to Lance out of reflex to demand to know if he knew what was going on with her. When Lance didn't return, his shoulders hunched up and he crossed his arms, isolating himself as he looked back at Adrianna who was not done.

"She's dying," she told him.

"Again?" Adam relaxed at that, almost letting out a laugh. "She's always dying. She was dying for years with the—"

"Her heart is gone," Adrianna continued, solid and firm and fighting back the emotion that the words were stirring in her. "Someone in Wonderland took it out and is keeping it there."

"So someone finally found out," Lance said, looking almost relieved.

Adrianna rounded on him, furious. She could feel the tears come back, the flush forming in her cheeks, but she didn't care. For the moment, despite knowing better, he looked like her brother and her brother had been keeping something very important from her. "You *knew?*" she demanded. "And you didn't tell me?"

"I failed to protect her," he said in a way that reminded her that he wasn't Lance. That reminded her specifically that he was not her brother at that moment and he would not be taking the scorn for her words. "And in return I kept her secret."

"Why?"

"She was content," he said. "And she made me promise. She said it made everyone else happy. That they were better off with her like this. I tried to reason with her, but she was very insistent that she was fine."

"*This* is your debt you have to repay?" Arthur demanded. "You're staying for *this?*"

"Yes. And she *is* correct that she can't get back on her own. Morgana called her over and took her heart. I couldn't stop her, though I did try. So I've stayed to watch over her and keep her secret until such time as someone else was able to realize it."

Even Adam was rolling his eyes, though she could see the fury building up in him. "And if she dies, what happens to Wonderland?" he demanded.

"No one cares about Wonderland!" Adrianna yelled at him. "Are you going to help me keep her from dying or not?"

"Her death saves Wonderland," Cat said appearing in the corner of the room. He was close to Adam, though Cat did not look pleased to see him so much as he was interested in Adrianna and her rage. "And you cannot get back. Only she can, if she can remember how she traveled there before. Unfortunately, she may mistake her door for a rabbit hole if she does that. So confused, the poor thing must be. Stealing other people's doors and not knowing what her own is."

"What are you doing here?" Adam snapped at him.

"Who is this?" Arthur asked, peering at the purple-haired boy that was now before him. "How did you get in here?"

"Did this one lose his manners with his hand?" Cat asked no one at all. "A terrible place to store manners, though perhaps they were kept there to make an impression. A shame he's lost them all. Perhaps he should focus on getting those back. If he can find them again. Unless, of course... No, this one would not have given anything away. Likely just left his hand behind somewhere and had forgotten where he left it."

Arthur moved forward, but Lance was there to stop him. He held Arthur back while Cat stayed still, sipping a drink loudly through his straw. "You will never truly understand what happened," Cat said, more to Adrianna than anything else, though his eyes flickered to Adam. "Perhaps it will choose you next. The Caterpillar certainly has. And it's his plan that we are relying on now. After all, you didn't protect the boy and Morgana's gotten him as well."

"What?" Adam demanded. "I was never supposed to—"

"She asked you to protect the boy," Cat told him. "Or have you fallen so much for a different warrior woman that you have forgotten what your princess has asked of you? Protect the boy and we would have had more time. You did not and numbers have run off the clocks. We have already broken the clocks we could find, but time continues to run out more and more quickly. Now we need to find something drastic else to save our world. This comes down on you."

"I wasn't supposed to protect Peter," Adam insisted. "No one told me to. The Caterpillar would have—"

"You argue, but it does no good," he said. "You have already lost. You failed your task. And now she has to die. We do not have time left. But perhaps Wonderland will choose you next. Once her heart is useless, Wonderland will have to find another. And maybe if you are better at staying away from Wonderland than Alice is, then you will save us."

"What's going on?" Adrianna demanded. Too many things were being said and she understood none of them. "You said— This is all because *Peter's* gone?"

Arthur chimed in, putting the madness together. "Morgana wants the magic for herself. Avalon isn't there anymore, but it's been split into Wonderland and Neverland. So she's going to take them both apart and put them back together in her image. When she does, she's going to be too powerful to stop. But to do that, she needs whoever the worlds chose, whatever makes those worlds what they are. And what makes Wonderland what it is is Alice. And Peter, he made Neverland, didn't he?"

Adrianna nodded. That much information she had been privy to from dealing with Alice and Peter herself. Peter had admitted that he didn't know how anything in Neverland worked, only that whatever he wanted appeared. It was a world made entirely by his imagination. She didn't know how Wonderland was assembled, but she could believe that somehow Alice had made Wonderland.

"So she has them now," Arthur said. "And that means it's time for her to take them apart and put them back together."

"But she only has Alice's heart."

"That's all she needs," Adam said. "Wonderland is driven by those. You've seen what happens. She doesn't need the rest of Alice. So all we need to do is let Alice die and Wonderland is safe. Right?"

"Adam!"

"That is true," Cat said. "A sad truth. And one I would rather not have come to pass. But one that you have permitted. You and that Caterpillar. He is not one of us, but he has been the only one with a plan and sometimes a plan is all you need to decide what to play next. Wonderland was fun once. Now, I would rather it were less interesting."

He looked off to the side staring at nothing at all and

going very still. His purple eyes went very wide, the drink in his hand slipping and the straw falling out of his mouth.

Adrianna ignored his sudden inattention as she rounded on him. "You need to take us over there. Right now."

"I shan't," Cat said. "You will find your own way, dear. But for right now, I must go."

"At least show Alice how to get back through the mirrors," Lance said. "So we can go and save her where you can't."

"Not today. I have another place to be, another thing to do."

"Where are you going?"

"I only promised that I would not allow her back," Cat said with a sly grin. "I am quite content that she uses her own door from now on. And it seems she has."

"But where are you going?"

"To one last tea party."

He vanished before them, and Adrianna could swear she could see a tail as he vanished. Not that it mattered as his words landed and registered. She said nothing before she bolted out of the room, running up to their dorm room and bursting in. There was no one left behind in the bed, the covers still there and a book left behind on the covers like the reader had gotten distracted and wandered off. Which, she was sure, Alice had.

CHAPTER 21

The White Book

ADRIANNA WAS IN a panic the next day, but she was determined to make this work. She gave up on her classes and closed herself off to everyone, missing more than one of her midterms as she threw herself into the white book. Adam and even Arthur had tried to convince her to go back to her normal life, to at least sit for tests, but she was too concerned with looking for a way to find Alice.

Dying. She was *dying*. She could already be dead and Adrianna wouldn't even know it.

It was Sarah that finally barged into her room at the end of the school day. Adrianna didn't realize she had left it unlocked. Usually Alice would check the locks and make sure that no one would come in and see anything when they were working with the books, but there was no Alice anymore. She needed to remember these things on her own, or get Alice back so she wouldn't need to.

Adrianna didn't stop her from coming in, gesturing only for her to close the door before she looked back down at the white book. She had the answer, at least. She found a way. Now she only needed to come up with a place to start.

It only hurt when Sarah sat across from her, sitting on Alice's bed. Out of the corner of her eye, she could almost imagine Alice was still there when she did that. But when she looked up, Sarah was too different from her, like someone dressing up as her. She was still too vibrant and alive, her blonde hair neatly done in braids and pins on her head, her makeup flawless and her attire perfectly in place.

It was like what Alice was like just before she disappeared. Which, now that she thought about it, was very unlike Alice at all.

"Are you okay?" Sarah asked, watching her carefully and her eyes falling on the tome in Adrianna's lap. "Addie, you haven't eaten. Come join us for dinner at least. What's going on?"

"Alice is missing," she said. She could say more to Sarah. Sarah knew some of what was going on, at least, and she wouldn't think Adrianna was crazy. She might know what to do. Adrianna couldn't have the police involved in this. They wouldn't be able to do anything. And she couldn't deal with everything else. She needed to get her back. "She was dying and now she's missing. I need to find her, to get her back before…"

"Hug?" Sarah offered. She came closer with her arms out in offer. Adrianna took it, glad to have the comfort. She squeezed tight and she could feel herself starting to hurt. "It's okay," Sarah said quietly. "Go ahead."

With the permission, the stress of the last day came rushing out in a torrent of tears. "Why didn't she tell me?" Adrianna asked, not sure she would ever get an answer. "Was I that bad? Why wouldn't she just tell me?"

"It's Alice," Sarah said in a way that was meant to be comforting. "She has a hard time letting anyone know she's having a hard time. She doesn't want anyone to worry about her. And you know you would have worried. And she doesn't want anyone to save her, and that's what you do."

"But she didn't tell me," Adrianna said. "She always tells me."

Sarah held back something, but Adrianna knew what it was. Alice had stopped telling her a long time ago. She had never been completely honest, and then she had stopped telling her altogether when she had questioned her. It was so hard to be her friend, but Alice couldn't help but be endearing. She was having such a hard time and was so strong during it all. And Adrianna wanted to help her so she wouldn't also have to be so alone. But she was so good at being alone.

"She had her heart taken," Adrianna told her as she tried to wipe away her tears. It was good to tell someone who would react appropriately and Sarah looked appropriately shocked. "She hasn't had it for ages and she hid it from me. And I didn't even notice that she was sick. I thought it was just midterms. She said she had a cold or the flu or something. And she seemed fine. She was happy, wasn't she? I thought she was finally getting to be normal. I should have noticed."

"You were busy," Sarah said. "Arthur takes a lot of attention."

"It wasn't even Arthur. I was only going out with him because he did something to Lance so that he's not even Lance anymore. And *Lance* kept it from me too."

Sarah said nothing, continuing to offer soothing pats and urging her to keep going if she needed to. And Adrianna needed to.

"I should have noticed. That cough has been going for so long. And she's been getting tired. She should have seen a doctor."

"She wouldn't go to a doctor and you know it." She took a deep breath and kept silent for a moment while she patted Adrianna on the back. She didn't relax and finally pulled away, putting her hands on Adrianna's shoulders. "Look, I know I said I didn't want to get involved anymore and I really don't. This whole thing seems like a mess, but... Addie, where did Alice really go? What's going on? Tell me everything. One thing at a time from the beginning."

"It's..." Adrianna didn't know what she would do or say, her mind spinning. "She wouldn't..."

There was a single sharp knock at the door before it opened. Adam appeared in the doorway and paused at the sight of Sarah sitting there. He stared at her and Adrianna knew he was thinking the same things that Adrianna had. That it looked for just a moment like Alice was back, but also that she was so much unlike Alice.

But then he saw the red face of his sister, of the tears that she was now trying to wipe away. He went still and Adrianna thought when he opened his mouth, he might excuse himself and leave to avoid dealing with her tears.

"I need to talk to my sister," Adam told her firmly. He looked uncomfortable.

"Sure." Sarah did not get up or leave or move at all.

"Alone."

"You're going to have to wait," Sarah said. "I'm not going anywhere."

"It's okay," Adrianna said. "She's... she knows some of it, anyway."

"I know barely any of it," Sarah pointed out. "But I'll listen. I won't do anything, probably, but I'll listen."

"Get out," Adam said.

"Or you'll try to sacrifice me to the Bandersnatch too?" Sarah asked.

The color drained from Adam's face and the bite fell out of his words. "What?"

"Yeah, I know about that," Sarah told him, inching away from Adrianna to round on Adam. "I was in there for a while, too. Ask Evan about it. I waited for Alice to save me and I saw a lot while I was in there. And I know about Wonderland."

"You don't know what really happened in there," Adam said, though he looked more desperate than sure of himself. "She wouldn't do anything. I had to. And she stopped me and—"

"And it sounds like it was a good thing," Sarah snapped back at him, getting to her feet and into his face about it. "*She* got everyone out."

"And screwed over Wonderland!"

"And made sure she didn't get herself stuck in that garden!" Sarah roared back at him. "Do you know what it's like to be in there? Just waiting to see if he is coming to take just a nibble off of you. Not able to do anything. *Can't* do anything. You start to go *insane* after a while. Your brother might have gotten out after a couple months, but I was stuck in there *for a year!* And everyone else was there longer! You would screw them all over just for Wonderland?"

"*Yes.*"

"Fuck you." Sarah was furious and red and stormed out of there, forgetting about Adrianna entirely as she pushed past the other people hovering outside the door. Adrianna looked and thought again of Alice and how she would always be the one to make sure it was private when Wonderland came up. But again, she was lucky as Arthur and Lance appeared at the door, both of them looking in at Adam and shaking their heads. Adrianna wiped her eyes and went back to the white book. They were all here. That saved her the trouble. It was time to get going.

"So someone's finally chewed you out," Arthur said. "A little lighter than I would have hoped. It would have been fun to watch something that small knock you on your ass."

"Get in," Adrianna instructed them. She wiped her eyes and took in a deep breath. "Close the door. It's time to go."

"Go?" Arthur asked. He looked at the book in her lap, his expression changing drastically. "Where did you get that?"

"Alice," Adrianna said. Lance closed the door behind them and Adrianna got up to make sure it was locked. "You stay as Lancelot for a little longer. Keep my brother safe. I don't know what we're going to do there, but I need you to help me get Alice back."

"Where did *she* get that book?" Arthur asked, moving toward it. Adam grabbed him by the arm to pull him back. "Do you even know what that is?"

Adrianna's hands cut through the air, her eyes closed as she thought of the inside of the White Rabbit's house. It was the only place in Wonderland she could think of that might be safe, and every part of her wanted to go there. She wanted them all to go. Needed them to follow her there. She could feel the spell push back, could feel it trying to keep her away, but she was not going to let it stop her.

"Addie! What are—"

"*Hie ætgenámoon.*"

The world around them fell away and they all vanished. She hoped when they reappeared, they would be in Wonderland.

Chapter 22

Smoke and Magic

ARTHUR WASN'T IMPRESSED as they appeared scattered ten feet apart from one another. "What on earth do you think you're doing?" he demanded. "You're lucky you didn't kill us all with that! You can't just say some words from a book and hope it's going to work!"

"It did work, though," Lance said, grinning and pulling Arthur back.

At least they were in Wonderland. Adrianna looked around and found that there was a lake in front of them, sparkling pink with two boys arguing on the opposite shore. Adrianna couldn't hear what it was, only the tone in their voice and the look in Adam's eyes as he took in the sights.

He took a deep breath of Wonderland and looked around, looking like he had finally accomplished a lifelong dream.

In a way he had, and he had been willing to be awful to accomplish that. She knew he would never want to leave again.

Adrianna grabbed him before he could run, holding his arm tightly and staring him down. "No matter what happens," she warned him, "I will find you again. Please, Adam. Just help me save her."

Adam looked back at her and tugged his arm out of her grasp. He looked back from her to Arthur for just a moment and back to her, his mind turning and trying to rationalize it. "If I help you get it back, Morgana can't use it to destroy Wonderland." He waited for Arthur to appear to agree, but Lance stepped in first.

"That would be what the Cheshire Cat mentioned," Lance said. "So far they haven't been able to get it back from Morgana. Can you?"

A grin formed across Adam's face. "Oh yeah," he said, looking around. "I'll need a distraction. Come on, I need my supplies and a few people. Come with me." There was something about him as he turned, something happier and lighter. It was too much like how happy Alice was when she came back here and Adrianna couldn't understand it. This place was awful and clearly doing something terrible to them. He was about to rush into danger and he looked positively ecstatic about it.

But then again, this was Adam. He always looked happy about being in danger.

They followed him into the forest and Adrianna tried to pay attention to Wonderland and see what he saw in it. She had thought it would be a nicer world, one that was something that anyone would want to do. What she saw around her was strangeness, twisted and dark versions of her normal world, and a haze hovering over the sky that had been previously a brilliant blue. It was gray now, and looked like there was a very large part of darkness growing in one part of the sky. In the distance, there was night bleeding into the gray, draining the color and light out of the world.

Around them, the world was also dark and strange. Things were growing twisted and she was sure that she wasn't seeing whatever drew Alice here. Something was here, something dark, and a presence lingered over the world. Parts of the foliage were vibrant and almost fluorescent compared to other places that looked drained and tired. Wandering about in the distance, she could see shambling shapes wandering around unconcerned with the trespassers in the forest. She didn't know what to make of it.

Adam led them somehow to a tea party deep in the forest. "You wander and it finds you," Adam said, making Adrianna no less concerned. He looked so determined that she didn't think he was wandering so aimlessly. Still, so long as there was a plan in place. As long as they had the people they needed to get Alice's heart back, it didn't matter.

The group around the table didn't look that formidable. She remembered the Mad Hatter from the last time she was here, and a few other people and animals wearing bits and pieces of Victorian clothing. Her attention went to a Caterpillar sitting at one corner of the table, as large as a cat and smoking a hookah that spewed out smoke of different colors and shapes. The smell of it was sweet and strangely comforting, but it tickled at her throat and she tried not to breathe it in so deeply.

She almost didn't register the person who stood up first, but it was definitely Tiger Lily who stormed over to Adam and smacked him hard across the face. "You had one task! One! And what do you do? You let him come here!"

"That's not what I was supposed to do!" he yelled back at her, gesturing to the Caterpillar. "He told me all I had to do was get back here and keep things in order. Take the hearts! Get the hearts back! That's all I had to do!"

"*Ahhhhh,*" the Caterpillar said on the other side of the table, exhaling a large puff of smoke as he spoke. "So difficult to remember that the priorities shift. More difficult when he doesn't return to know when they do so. He has not returned to me for too long. And if he does not return, why would I have updated it?"

A thin stream of smoke escaped him and crept and snaked across the table. Adrianna saw where it was headed in an instant and jumped forward, her hands waving it wildly and trying to dissipate it. The Mad Hatter frowned at it as it snaked around Adrianna, doing nothing to help as it continued on its path across the table and even around Tiger Lily to its target.

The smoke swept up around Adam, swirling around him as he tried to defend himself from Tiger Lily. She was still furious about things even as it engulfed him in the smoke, backing away as the fog hid him from view and continuing to yell at him as if it weren't there.

"The hearts are no longer a problem!" Tiger Lily yelled back at him. "The Queen of Hearts is gone! You don't need to get the hearts back if there is no one left to take them! We are dealing with *another* mad queen and you only needed to keep a child from coming to Wonderland! A stupid child who is scared of his own lands and people! Who tried to make another save a world he created!"

"I…" Adam started, but he was already faltering as he inhaled the surrounding smoke. "I wasn't supposed to… Fine, it's done," he said finally as his eyes cleared, straightening up and looking much less scared of Tiger Lily's wrath. "Then we need to move onto the next plan. If she has Peter, then we need to make Alice's heart useless. That should be easy."

Next to her Arthur watched it happen and every muscle

in his body went rigid, looking ready to turn and leap across the table at the Caterpillar. Too much was happening at once that Adrianna was losing track of it all. She needed to focus on one thing. She needed to figure out one thing she could do.

Adam first, she decided. The smoke was doing something to Adam's head. Whatever that smoke was, she had to clear its effects out of her brother while she had the chance or he had the potential to be very dangerous. He'd already become very dangerous.

And Arthur was close.

"What are you talking about?" Tiger Lily demanded. Her eyes cut back to the other side of the table, only now noticing that the Caterpillar was doing something. She rounded on him, bringing out her hatchet and throwing it. It whistled as it whipped across the table and smashed into the hookah, shattering it into dust and sending the smoke flying out in a wall. "Enough ideas from you!" she yelled. "You cause nothing but trouble!"

There was a rolling of eyes and a shuffling of people reaching for their sleeves before Adrianna could see only smoke. "Must we do this again?" the Mad Hatter said from somewhere in the fog.

The panic surging in Adrianna was enough to push her to action. She didn't know what the smoke did when the Caterpillar wasn't smoking it, but she had seen what it had done to her brother already. She reached out and grabbed hold of both Adam and Arthur's arms and pulled them hard together. They stumbled into one another and Adrianna shoved at one back. She hoped that was enough.

Light wind swept in around them and the fog thinned. The Mad Hatter looked annoyed, as did everyone else, as he continued to wave the smoke away with minimal commitment. Tiger Lily passed behind him on her way back around the table, now holding her hatchet again and looking like she was getting ready to throw it again.

Adrianna saw through the thinning fog that she had shoved Arthur into Adam, Lance slipping away. Arthur shoved Adam away from him, wiping his mouth and turning wildly around until he spotted Adrianna. He was red and furious, but his voice was quiet. "What are you doing?" he demanded. "If you think—"

"This isn't the time," Lance told him, pulling him back from her. "You have something else to deal with first." He looked pointedly at the Caterpillar on the other side of the table, large and looking entirely too content as he watched the chaos happen around him. The mouthpiece of the hookah twirled in his hands and the hookah came back together, filled with smoke.

"You're alive," Arthur said, the anger at what had just happened not completely gone yet. Still, his surprise at seeing the Caterpillar was enough to at least make him sound like he might not try to kill someone. "You've been here all along. Where have you been? When did you escape the ice?"

Adrianna remembered Cat saying something about the Caterpillar not belonging, but she decided that wasn't as important as making sure her brother was all right. She went down to Adam's side and focused on the chaos that was Adam getting to his senses. Tiger Lily came back to see them, not willing to help him in the least.

"Adam?" she asked. "Are you okay?"

He looked confused and then horrified at himself. "I was going to kill her," he said as the reality of what he was prepared to do dawned on him. He looked up at Tiger Lily and Adrianna, settling on his sister and pleading with her to make this make sense. "Was I really going to kill her?"

"You were really planning to murder Alice of Wonderland," Tiger Lily assured him. "The Caterpillar may be the only one with a plan, but he has outworn his usefulness. If you wish to save her, you will come with me now. Your friends appear to be making enough of a distraction so they won't follow. We'll save her heart and return it to her. We will rescue Peter from her. And this will take the evil Queen's power from her. You'll come as well," Tiger Lily added to Adrianna. "You killed the last Queen. You can do it again."

Adrianna agreed, fully ready and capable of doing that.

She glanced back, not sure what was going on. She heard Arthur refer to the Caterpillar as Merlin and Lance met her eyes. Quietly, he nodded and shooed them on their way, shifting to block Arthur's view from their departure.

"What are we doing?" Adrianna asked, running alongside Tiger Lily and Adam as they plunged into the forest and towards the dark parts of Wonderland.

"You distract her," Tiger Lily said. "We will find the heart and free Peter. Keep her busy until we are complete."

CHAPTER 23

Matt of Neverland

THEY GOT TO Tiger Lily's place in a mercifully short run. Adrianna could only barely keep up and was heaving for breath when they finally came to a halt. She sat outside, trying desperately to try to catch her breath. Someone gave her water and she drank it down, but they left before she could thank them. Her lungs were still on fire and she hoped that Tiger Lily would stall Adam for a little longer.

"*Of course you were supposed to watch him!*" Tiger Lily continued to yell at Adam behind her. "Even if you didn't know what was happening, he's more a child than he appears. He needs someone to make him stay when things are difficult. *Trust you*. You insist I trust you, and you come back to me like this!"

She couldn't even hear Adam's protests as Tiger Lily went off on him, but she wasn't sure she wanted the distraction of their argument at all. She was in over her head and she knew it. In less than an hour, she had jumped into a world she knew nothing about and forced her brother to kiss someone she hated to break a spell she wasn't even sure was there. That she was right made no difference.

What was she even *doing* here? She didn't know what she was doing. She had no plan. Alice was missing and dying and she really didn't know how to stop any of that. This was all only a series of impulses, and they were terrible impulses so far. Even a day ago she would have done nothing like this.

Something about Wonderland brought out the worst in everyone.

But Tiger Lily, at least, had a plan. She knew how to get into the castle and she knew just where to go. They had tried to get Alice's heart back already and knew precisely where it was being kept. With Peter in there now, it was more difficult to get in, but with enough of a distraction she thought they could do it. And Adrianna had been the one responsible for the vines that now crawled throughout the castle. She thought maybe she could use them again.

"It's time to go," Tiger Lily said. She was beside Adrianna, offering a hand to help her up. "We must be quick before your brother decides that it would be better to let her die again."

"I don't want *anyone* dead!" Adam tried to protest. "I don't know what that was!"

"We have no time," Tiger Lily said. She and Adam now wore heavy coats, ones that were clearly filled with things they might find useful. She gave a smaller one to Adrianna, one that looked lighter but she took it anyway. "Nothing will keep you safe, but it will prevent some injury. Come on, there is a rabbit hole into the castle over here."

"But the castle moved."

"Yes."

Tiger Lily said nothing more as she brought them a short ways out of her village to a small grove of trees with strange, metal boxes growing in them. There was a large blue fridge sitting at the base of one and she pushed it. It resisted, but ultimately moved out of the way, revealing a hole in the ground.

Adam asked no questions before jumping down it. Adrianna soon followed him, keeping her eyes firmly shut and holding her breath to keep herself from screaming in the descent. What she found instead was the sensation of floating, like she was drifting instead of plunging downwards. It was almost like being carried on a gentle current into danger.

She cracked an eye open to see what was happening. Adam and Tiger Lily were silent on either side of her, checking the placement of various weapons and other items in their coats, not paying any attention to the other things that floated past. No care was paid to the intricate carpets that carried tea cups or symbols on cards. Not even a nod to the mouse that watched them as they passed, shaking its head and looking very disappointed.

Adrianna kept her eyes shut for the rest of the journey until Adam grabbed her arm to pull her out. They were inside the castle, somewhere that made little sense to be. She could see out the window that they made it to the inside of a parapet near the top of it and Adrianna went to the window while Adam helped Tiger Lily out, staring out at the sky above them and the world below.

The sky looked almost angry as the night and the gray fought one another. To one side, there was a wall of vines that Adrianna had grown that looked like it was barely holding back all the terrors of the night world. She could almost see dark shapes moving in the cracks trying to get through. On the other was a dull gray landscape, dotted with the occasional resistance of a bright color. Lines of people and animals held their lines around the castle, not moving an inch even as the forest beside them shifted and roared.

Beyond the castle and the vines, a large tree had taken root and was already tearing a new hole in the world. She could see a darker world poking in around it, one filled with night and twisted figures moving around in the darkness.

There had to be something she was missing. Alice was so willing to sacrifice herself for this place. Even Adam had been. She didn't understand it.

"Addie, stay close," Adam said. She tore herself away from watching Wonderland to follow them down the stairs. She could feel her heart pounding heavily in her chest and tried to force herself to think of something useful. Of how to make the vines move. Of how to send people far away. Of how to defend them so that they wouldn't need to use their coats at all.

As soon as they got down the stairs, Adrianna was overwhelmed. There were too many people, too many weapons, and all of them coming directly at them. Where Tiger Lily and Adam were almost calm in their approach, quietly disposing of them as they came one by one, Adrianna alternated between freezing in place and running up to join them as they pressed onward.

The castle passed by her in a panicked blur. Adrianna didn't know how many turns they made, how many rooms they went through, how many halls she saw. How many fallen she had walked past. How many of them were dead or just injured. When they found one hall that was empty, Adrianna almost didn't understand what was happening.

"The door at the end," Tiger Lily told her, pointing to

the other side of the hall. "You will distract her. We will get the heart."

Adrianna nodded dully and watched them go, slipping into another door in the hall and leaving her alone. She wrapped her arms around herself, trying to take a steadying breath. It was to save Alice. She had brought them here. She was the one that had put all of this in motion. And now, she was given direction and a thing to do.

She didn't know if she could do this, but she had to, didn't she? She walked slowly down the hall, dragging her feet. Every step felt heavier than the last. But she had brought this on herself and everyone else. She was here to try to save Alice. Somehow, this would save Alice. That's what she was here for.

Something tapped her lightly on her shoulder. Adrianna jumped, sure that something had come up to kill her. Her eyes darted around for what it was, her eyes quickly landing on a smiling boy.

"Hey sis. You need a hand?"

Adrianna couldn't believe what she was seeing. Matt was there. It was really him. After so many years, she finally found him. He looked almost just like he did when she last saw him.

Almost.

He was even younger than before somehow. He had shrunk to the point when he was just starting school, back so many years ago. He was still young, so young, too young to be here in the middle of so much. He looked at her like he didn't recognize her, taking her in as much as she was taking him in, but she knew it was him. That expression, that confused and devious expression, was something she knew too well.

"Are you here to save him too?" Matt asked. "The Lost Boys asked me to see if I could save their old leader. Apparently this Peter guy is still pretty important to them, even though he apparently abandoned them and left them all for dead. *But they're cowards and hiding right now.*"

Above them in the hall, heads poked out from behind the banners and high windows. There were only four of them, young boys that looked like they were in elementary school, though now she wondered if that was how old they really were. If Matt had stopped aging and gone backwards, there was no telling how old any of these kids were. But they came out of hiding nonetheless and showed themselves uncomfortably to her like she was about to turn into something dangerous.

"She doesn't get to come back with us," one of them said. "When Peter brought a girl back, she murdered everyone and destroyed Neverland."

"You know Wendy?" Adrianna asked. She had only heard of her, but the stories were all heartbreaking.

"She murdered everyone," the boy repeated. "And so will you. You don't get to come."

"Matt, we thought you were gone forever," Adrianna said, turning back on him. "I can't believe you're still alive. What are you doing here?"

"Saving Peter," he repeated. "Didn't you hear me? Come on Addie, you didn't used to be dumb like this."

"She doesn't get to come!" the boy said. "She's gonna kill us all just like Wendy! Girls are the worst!"

Adrianna looked behind them and saw something behind them. Guards. They would get caught if they did nothing.

Adrianna made a sharp gesture, words forming on her lips that came from panic rather than reason. Vines reached down from the ceiling, plucking them out of the ground and yanking them into the air, growing around them on the ceiling.

"Okay, maybe she can come," the boy said. "But you have to deal with her!"

"Sure, Rocky," Matt said, rolling his eyes. "Come on, he's over this way." He smiled, the only one on the ground and darting ahead so fast that he left a streak behind. He seemed to think better of it, his friends taking flight and following behind him, and he looped back to join Adrianna again and run more normally paced. Adrianna stared back at him and couldn't quite believe what she was seeing.

"Where have you *been*?" she asked. He looked fine, at

least, but there was something strange in his demeanor and the way he talked. It was like he really was a kid again, and like he had never grown up. He was exactly as he had been when he was six. He was immature and he didn't really care for anything around him beyond how it would contribute to his entertainment. Full of imagination and mischief, but without Adam and Lance to help him, he had found new friends to feed into his fantasies. And he had apparently developed a speed beyond what was normal.

"Neverland," he said. "It's been fun. There's zombies everywhere! And all sorts of stuff, but it's been different lately. Things aren't making as much sense. It's weird. But we'll fix that when we take down Mor—Claudia."

"Take down who?" Adrianna asked, not sure what was going on. The boys around him seemed to think it was real and true, but she wasn't following. "Morgana?"

"And Claudia," Matt said. "They're the same person. She had a secret identity as an evil witch all along."

Adrianna hesitated, not sure how much more information she could get out of him or if it would really be worth it. She was already wary of what he was saying, not sure if any of this was going to be remotely useful later or accurate. Alice hadn't mentioned that Morgana was her stepmother, nor had anyone else. But, then again, Alice had kept the fact that her heart was missing from her. And this secret stung less.

What was happening to them? Didn't Alice trust her anymore? She was just trying to help her, to get her to think ahead to the future and to what she was going to be missing if she spent all her time and attention on Wonderland. It would leave her eventually and when it did, she needed to be ready. That was all. Dependency on this terrible place was getting to all of them.

"You have to come back," Adrianna said. "After this is all over, after it's done, we have to take you back. You can't stay here."

A grin appeared on Matt's face, defiant and daring her to try to do something. "Can't make me," he said, dashing forward and out of reach. Adrianna considered trying to make him, to use the magic to catch him and make him come back. She could do it with Adam, but now was not the time with Matt. She could figure it out once they had finished here. It would all work out. Eventually. She just needed time to figure it out and she didn't have that now.

"She's in here," Matt said, indicating the large door at the end of the hall and ushering Adrianna to get over there faster. He was still smiling widely, still proud of himself as he looked around, still watching nothing and pleased with himself. His friends were in awe of him. He looked so happy.

Adrianna rushed to meet them at the door. "Be careful,"

she said. "You don't have to do this, Matt. You could just wait here. We'll all go home together."

"I'll save him, don't worry," Matt said, rolling his eyes wide and comically again. He wasn't listening to Adrianna at all, addressing only the boys around them. "You don't have to come with me. I will deal with it while you *cowards* stay out here and make sure nothing else comes in. I'll just have to use my *sister* instead. Because a girl is better at this than any of you."

"Okay!" The boy, Rocky, said, sounded positively delighted with this plan.

Matt let out a heavy, exaggerated sigh and tugged Adrianna with him. "Come on, Addie. We need to go kill a witch."

CHAPTER 24

Sacrifice

ADRIANNA NARROWLY KEPT Matt from bursting through the door, pulling him behind her and pushing the door open more carefully. It was strange, that he was once older than she was and now she was treating him like a child. But Matt *was* a child now. A happy child about to walk into something terrible.

The door came open easily and she didn't know what to make of what she was seeing. The parts of it made sense in a movie, but not all in one piece. There were symbols drawn on the floor and on the ceiling. Herbs hung randomly, making it smell much like Claudia's office at home. Adrianna didn't know the intricate patterns, or what the sheets scattered around the sides of the room and covering the small side tables were, but Morgana had been doing a great deal of work on them, covering them in writing and drawings.

To one side, she spotted what she had come for. Sitting on a strange altar wrapped in thorny vines, there was a box made of glass, one that was marked with a small black headband like Alice used to wear and the initials AL. Inside, still beating, was a heart that didn't have a trace of blood on it, unlike Lance's heart had. I was more like those of Wonderland. It beat stronger than she thought it would, but the color from it was draining. It was still the most vibrant thing in this room, brilliantly red against the stone and symbols and dried vegetation.

On the other side of the room, hanging from the ceiling by his arms with a set of vines, Peter was unconscious and looking much worse for wear. His clothes had tears in several places. The blood she could see had dried onto his skin and his torn clothing turned a dull brown from the stains. He looked like he had already been through enough things, but she couldn't see a single cut or bruise actually on him. Despite that, she could see the circles around his eyes looking so dark she might mistake them for injuries if she weren't looking in such close horror.

Pacing in front of him, looking at her notes, was her stepmother. Claudia looked different now. Her hair was down and she still looked uncannily like she had stolen Adrianna's face. A beauty, to be sure, and Adrianna had once wanted to emulate her. But the woman standing there wasn't Claudia, not anymore. It was a woman named Morgana and she needed to be stopped.

"Unhand him!" Matt demanded loudly. Adrianna had almost forgotten he was there and jumped at his declaration.

Morgana barely turned, waving her hand at Matt. He vanished next to her, leaving Adrianna standing alone to face her stepmother. Her heart clenched inside her chest, her mind racing through all the things that might have happened to Matt. He could be in a dungeon, or surrounded and out-numbered, or back in Neverland. He could be anywhere. He could even be…

No, there was no time to think about that, was there? She couldn't panic now. It would be just as easy to get rid of her, and she was now alone. She wouldn't be much of a distraction if that happened. She had to deal with Morgana or Claudia or whoever she was before she dealt with the fact that her brother had just vanished.

Her eyes flickered to the heart and something appearing near it. She saw that someone was there, a glimpse of Adam and Tiger Lily crawling along the higher parts of the walls and hidden among the herbs, communicating quietly and furiously about the best way to get the heart now that they had found it. A glance from Tiger Lily to Adrianna telling her she had a job to do. It was time to keep the evil Queen's attention away from the heart while they grabbed it.

But Morgana's attention was already being pulled away from whatever it was she was doing. In her glance that swept Matt away, it seemed she had seen something else and she turned back now, getting a look at the other Adrianna standing there so quietly. She developed an odd expression, curious and not angry but surprised as she faced Adrianna. "Well hello," Morgana said. "And what brings you here?"

And she *was* Morgana now. Her stepmother wasn't around any longer, now leaving behind only this woman who wanted to do them harm and cause them problems. And Alice would suffer the end of it if she didn't do something about it. A distraction. She needed to be a distraction.

"Hi," Adrianna started, hoping more ideas would come to her. But she had to come up with something. She had never been quick like her brothers, but she knew how to cause a distraction for them if she ever needed to. "Why are you here?" she asked, changing her expression to be one of surprise and shock and awe. "Aren't you Claudia? You disappeared."

"I was never really Claudia," Morgana told her. "My name's always been Morgana, but your father liked Claudia more."

"You changed your name for him?"

"We all do silly things for love."

She could see Adam and Tiger Lily creeping closer. "But

why are you here?" she asked. She needed to keep her attention.

"I'm trying to bring my home back. And perhaps you would like to come. I suppose you would want to when I'm done. Avalon really is a wonderful place, even if it doesn't favor me anymore. It might not even if I bring it back, but that's okay." She let out a deep sigh, the smile on her face turned wry. "But it's not ready yet. Go back home, Adrianna. I'll call you when it's time."

"Can I take Peter with me?" she asked, walking further into the room and trying to keep her eyes away from the heart. She moved wide around the room and stared past Morgana to Peter, trying to tell if he was still breathing at least. He looked limp and so cold. "I know him. I go to school with him. He shouldn't be here."

Morgana frowned. "No, he shouldn't be," she muttered, not sure what to make of him as she looked back at Peter. "Tell me, Addie, where is this boy from? I thought he was the one I needed, but I can't seem to figure out how to get what I need out of him."

"He's just Peter," Adrianna said, inching closer and trying to think. Slowly, her fingers twitched and the vines in the rest of the castle listened to her, coming up through the cracks in the floor at her call. They wound around Morgana's feet and Adrianna hoped they would grow fast enough to catch her while she wasn't paying attention. "That's Kevin's brother. What did you think he was?"

"The key to Neverland," she muttered, stepping away. She put a foot on one vine and it crumbled to dust beneath her foot, though she said nothing about it. Adrianna could tell she knew of what she was doing and dismissing it as she regarded Peter. She picked up his face as he hung. He let out a light groan at her touch. "None of this is turning out to be as easy as I hoped. Neither of you are very cooperative."

Peter sneered, but he looked much too weak all strung up like that to do anything about it. His bleary eyes settled on Adrianna and then Morgana, and then back to Adrianna, confusion rampant on his face. "Not mine…" he said, looking like he was ready to pass out again. "Not mine…"

"I'm starting to believe you," Morgana said. "Who did you give it to?"

Peter glared back at her, looking like he would do something rash, and Adrianna stomped forward, making enough noise to gain her attention. With the eyes now on her, she looked around and back to Peter, and more pointedly not at Alice's heart. Out of the corner of her eye, Adrianna could see movement as they were making their move.

Keep her talking. Just keep her talking.

"Have you seen what I can do?" Adrianna asked, moving around her. She couldn't get close enough to turn her to stone, but the vines were still listening and waiting for her to give them some direction. A distraction. She needed to be a distraction right now. She could see Tiger Lily split off from Adam and creep in closer to get Peter out. Adrianna needed to be a distraction. By any means necessary.

"*Þá ymbsetenna geníepe!*"

It had worked on the Queen of Hearts. Adrianna cast the spell like she had done so long ago, bringing her hands down as the vines shot up from the ground to engulf her. She couldn't bring nearly the malice to her actions as she had with the Queen of Hearts. She couldn't bring the same anger into the spell as she had before, and the vines did not feed from her like they had before. This woman might be Morgana, the witch who had taken Alice's heart and kidnapped Peter, but she was also Claudia, a stepmother who did nothing mean to her.

Morgana barely flinched as the vines swallowed her. A moment later, a flame flickered into existence at the top of the vines and fell down around her in a ring, burning the vines away. She looked only annoyed as she regarded Adrianna.

"And this is why I had to adjust you," she said, her hand moving. Adrianna didn't see the vines grow up around her until it was too late, picking her up and holding her a few feet off the ground. They wound around her, tightly enough to keep her still but not uncomfortable unless she struggled.

Adrianna could see the thorns had all avoided being pointed directly at her, but would scratch her if she struggled. "Don't worry, Addie, I won't harm you. I was quite fond of all of you kids. But it's time for me to return home. Once I figure out how to put home back together."

On the other side of the room, she could see Adam working his way closer to the box. His fingers ran delicately over the vines keeping the box in place and the thorns that protected it, taking something out of his pocket and sawing at them. He cut them away one by one, shooting a look back at Adrianna that was between concern and anxious for her to do something.

"You did something to me?" Adrianna asked Morgana. She didn't really care what she might have done, not while she was trying to keep her captive, but she needed to keep her occupied and distracted. Keep her from seeing what was going on behind her. "Why?"

"An ambitious young girl, you were," she said. "Too smart for your own good. And you were talented. And we couldn't have another of those in that house."

The flash came out of nowhere and Adrianna couldn't help but look. Out of nowhere, a circle of ice rose around the heart, around the entire case as Adam was just about done cutting it free. She could see a few red drops dripping off of the tip of one icicle, dribbling down the side. Adam was on the ground, his eyes cutting across the room to Morgana, then to the intruder at the door.

There was a girl standing there, eyes black as her hair and skin almost paler than Adrianna's. She watched the room, spending only a moment on Adam as he shrunk away from her. She even passed her attention over Morgana and Adrianna, her eyes falling squarely on Peter before she spoke. "You have intruders. You should be more careful."

"It seems I do," Morgana murmured. Her expression became puzzled as she looked at Adam, the vines whipping up around him and grabbing him. He tried to run, but the vines were faster, grabbing him and growing into roses and thorns around him to keep him firmly in place. "Adam," she said. "Are you all coming to see me? I didn't mind most of the children, but you were always the most trouble of them all. You and Matt, neither of you would ever quite behave properly."

"Lance always was the good one," he told her, struggling to get out. The thorns, Adrianna noticed, moved gently out of the way as he moved, catching on his clothes but never giving him more than a warning and never drawing blood when they could. "Let me go!"

"Loud intruders," she said. "Boys always are. I can take him if you'd like. And Peter, if you're done with him. And her. I've never seen what the inside of a girl looks like before. The last one ran away before I could see."

"Almost done," Morgana said. "Though you'll be leaving the other two alone."

"Why?" Her eyes drifted away from Peter and around to Morgana. Adrianna wasn't sure she had seen her blink yet. "Are they important?"

"They were my children in another life," Morgana said. "That's Adam and this is Adrianna."

Wendy regarded Adrianna, eyes wide and crawling over her torso instead of her face. "Will you teach her things too? I think I would like her better if I could see inside her first. Make sure she didn't take Peter from me too. I'd only need a moment. Or a few moments. I only—"

There were two overlapping heavy thuds and another flash. Adrianna recognized Peter falling to the ground, the vines holding his arms in place severed and Tiger Lily still nowhere in sight. A series of jagged spears of ice jutted out from around the ground behind him, but there was no sign of anything there as she scanned the room.

"Wendy, you should be more careful," Morgana scolded her, her tone gentle.

"Why?" she asked, her eyes on Peter again. "I can put him back if I break him. He's still small. Will he have the squishy thing for Michael do you think?"

"He may have a kidney that will fit," Morgana said.

"And then I'll do what you did. I'm just going to take his heart and keep it for myself."

"You'll never find who has Neverland without me," Peter said, his voice strained as he tried to push himself off the ground. His hands stayed bound and he still slumped forward, but his bleary eyes were up and trained on Morgana. "You can't get rid of me yet."

"Unraveling that heart is a much better use of my time," Morgana said, drifting over to it as a frown reappeared across her features. "That girl's done something to it. Perhaps Wendy's free to talk to you and if she can get you to say anything, all the better."

"That's *Alice's* heart. She's going to die if you do anything to it."

Tears stung Adrianna's eyes, staring out at what was happening and trying to pull herself free. She couldn't do anything, couldn't find the words to join in Peter's plea to leave Alice's heart alone. Even Adam was pulling harder at his vines and the scratches on his arms grew deeper, though they grew stronger around him to keep him still.

"What do you care about Alice?" Wendy asked in front of Adrianna, her body rigid as she looked at Peter. Adrianna could only imagine the look on her face, hearing the betrayal and anger in her tone.

But Peter didn't, his attention still on Morgana. "She's not even here to defend herself. You can't even get in anyway. I can take it back to her. Maybe if you ask her really nice, she can give Wonderland to someone else that you can—"

It happened all in an instant. There was another flash, another series of spikes of ice coming out of the ground, this time directly under Peter. This time there was much more than just a drop of blood that poured down the slope of ice. But Peter was safe.

Tiger Lily pushed Peter out of the way before any of them could see what was happening, Tiger Lily's body was in the air with ice sticking through it in far too many places. The largest was in her chest and the ice was as red as the rest of the castle outside this room. She didn't move. Her head fell to the side and her eyes stared at nothing. Her coat was covered in a light layer of frost, melted only where the bright red dribbled down to melt it.

The yells around the room were loud and echoed through the room. Adam tore himself free of the vines that held him, hacking them apart as he drove himself forward to her. Peter watched from the floor and stared wide eyed at the woman who had just gotten in the way to save him. Adam kept looking at her, hesitating to touch her, to check and see if she was okay. She was not okay. She was not alive. He knew it, but he didn't want it to be true.

Tears stung Adrianna's eyes but she had to get them out of there. Morgana was dangerous and they were no match for her. Morgana didn't seem bothered, just watching as they mourned and grieved, waiting for them to turn on her. And she knew Adam would any moment. Adrianna had to move quickly to save both of them from his actions next.

She got her hand free, desperation alone making it possible. "*Hie ætgenámoon!*" she commanded, sweeping her hand out wide to make sure it caught Adam and Peter and Tiger Lily. She hoped that Arthur would know how to do something, that maybe he could fix it. That anyone could save her even though it was already too late.

As they disappeared, Adrianna saw something purple curl itself around the box with Alice's heart in it. They were gone before she could figure out if Cat was doing anything worthwhile.

CHAPTER 25

Tea Party

ALICE THOUGHT IT was a very nice send off. She knew this wasn't what anyone wanted, but she was getting so tired of living in a way that made others approve of her. She was good for her father, and her father was never happy. She had managed to become normal for Adrianna, and Adrianna had not been happy. There was nothing she could do to make them happy with her. She tried so hard, and yet it never seemed to be enough. And she was getting so tired of trying.

The White Rabbit sat there on the other side of her, watching her and waiting for her to take a seat. There was actual tea on this table, drinkable because it was a party not hosted by the Mad Hatter. She took her seat with him and looked across the table to see the Cheshire Cat also sitting atop the table, nursing a cup of his own. Not tea, but a slurpee that he still insisted drinking from a loud straw.

"About time," the White Rabbit said kindly. "We so hoped that it didn't have to come to this. So unfortunate that it has."

"Come to what?" Alice asked.

"We hoped it would only be a game," the White Rabbit said. "But a good game is one that you can play again with the same friends. But it seems you will not be here for much longer."

"No," Alice said. "That's not what happens next."

"The Caterpillar's plan is a bad one," Cat insisted. "Death is not the answer and it will not be this time."

"Death is such a terrible subject for tea."

"Perhaps you shouldn't have invited the dying to tea," Alice said.

"I do not want you to die," the White Rabbit said. "And you may not yet. No matter how much you may want to yourself, you would be greatly missed."

"I don't want to die," Alice insisted.

"Oh, of course not," Cat said, every word sarcastic. "Alice, the girl who waits patiently for death to come to her because she is trying so hard not to be rude to death. If anyone deserves rudeness, it is the Reaper. Taking friends and enemies alike as if they were the same thing."

"What should I do?" Alice asked. "I can't make anyone happy. And when I do make them happy, they get mad at how

I'm doing it. Much better if I should let them find their own way without trying to please them. No one ever asks what Alice wants."

"Not even Alice," Rabbit pointed out. "Do you know why it is Cat and I are here with you now?"

"No."

"Because we were like you once," he said. "Wonderland finds children lost in their daydreams and gives them a home. But you have stopped dreaming. Perhaps it was a bad idea to bring you back, but I do hope you've remembered how to daydream again."

"I don't want to."

"But you do," Cat told her. "Or you would have never found your way back again. Finally doing something for yourself, even if it is something that we wanted. And perhaps you must learn how to live for yourself. We will never tell you what you must do."

"That's all you do."

"That is all we do," Rabbit agreed, a smile spreading across his face as he topped up the cups. "But we do not mean for you to listen. It is so strange to see you do that. You fought so much harder before. We have missed that. You can fight again. We will not be mad."

"We will always be mad. That is the point."

"It wouldn't be Wonderland without the madness," Alice

said. "That was always the problem. No one else wanted me to be mad."

"Did you want to be mad?"

Alice stayed quiet. "It's not about what I want," she said finally. "My father puts a roof over my head and pays my tuition, so I need to do what he wants. Adrianna is my friend, so the least I can do is to try and make her happy. Wonderland asks things of me, and it won't leave me alone until I fulfill everything it asks."

"You could have passed Wonderland along to someone else whenever you wanted," the White Rabbit reminded her. "The other boy did it with Neverland, and that was his whole world. You could have left whenever you wanted."

"But you liked me."

"We still like you."

"I will return," Cat said, his ears perking up and curious. His eyes narrowed and his fur was puffed up. "And when I do, you will have a choice."

"I don't want to know, do I?" Alice asked.

"If you wanted to know, you should have asked. Questions are always welcome and you used to be full of them. I don't know what they did on that side, but I imagine it was awful."

"It's fine," Alice said.

"So you say."

"It is!"

"So you say."

Alice studied the Rabbit and pondered over it. "If you try to tell me to do anything, you'll be just the same," Alice said. "Everyone tells me what to do. I don't get to decide for myself. I make bad choices. It's for the best that way."

"So you say."

Alice wasn't even mad. She couldn't be. She was just tired and fighting back another round of coughing. It would be rude to cough and get blood all over this nice tablecloth. At least the tea was soothing on her throat. She wondered when the table had gotten a tablecloth, but Rabbit didn't look concerned as he took another sip of his tea.

He watched her carefully and his expression was somber. This felt like her wake. It probably was.

Cat reappeared a moment later curled up in a very puffy ball. His eyes were ones of curiosity as they watched her carefully, ready to gauge her reaction and decide if it was a good idea to give her this option. He moved his tail and stepped off of his treasure, revealing a glass box with Alice's heart inside of it.

Alice already knew what he had before he said or did anything. She could feel it. She felt stronger just being near it. The cough disappeared from her throat and the itching from her lungs. The beating echoed in her ears. That beating. Her beating.

There were still thorns around the box when Cat got off of it and pushed it across the table to her. As it drew closer, she felt warmer and more herself. More alive. Her hands warmed and her legs didn't feel so weak. None of her felt dizzy anymore just by having it close. She was already better. She was...

She could also hear the rest of it coming back along with the thrumming in her ears. The madness and the pain. The headache was already there, and the feeling of slowly unraveling. She could barely concentrate, feeling the world around her calling to her and trying to lure her back into it.

"Your choice, Alice dear," Cat said somberly, stepping away from the box. "You can take your heart back and try to save Wonderland, or you can save Wonderland by destroying it. We will not stop you. It will be your choice."

Alice stared at the box, running her finger around the edges and thinking about it hard. She could feel it so close to beating in her chest again. It was calling her, begging to come back to the safe cocoon of her ribcage. She could be alive again, truly alive and aware. She would be able to run and jump and experience life. Food would taste right and she wouldn't wake up with a cough.

More than that, she would live.

But what life would it be? Again, Wonderland would demand that she did whatever it wanted. The madness would seep in again and her relationships would fall apart. She would have to fight them when she went back, trying harder and harder to keep herself silent so that the madness wouldn't slip out. When she went home, she would be alone again for months and unable to see anyone. And when she did see them and they wanted her to talk, it would only be madness that came out.

More than that, Alice was still beholden to Wonderland, forced to come back again and again to save it from things she did not cause for a promise she never made. It was a life where she would only continue to disappoint everyone around her. And the people not around her. She had already let Wonderland down by letting her heart get caught, by not returning the hearts, by not doing anything to help it and actively trying to ignore it.

She kept running her fingers over it until she found the drop of red. Blood was here. She touched it and pulled her hand away, letting her eyes linger on it a little longer. "What happened?" Alice asked, not looking away from the red between her fingers. "How did you come by my heart?"

"If he tells you, you will not be making the choice on your own."

"I choose to know," Alice said sadly, knowing what this meant.

And so Cat told her what he had seen.

CHAPTER 26

Fall to Flames

NOTHING COULD BE done to save Tiger Lily. The young woman was gone and would never come back, no matter how many people Adam threatened.

Her people took her body away and both Adam and Peter followed them. Adrianna lingered back, sitting with Lance and Arthur at a loss for what to do. The Caterpillar was a cocoon at the other side of the table and the rest of the party moved on, paying their respects before getting back to the business of deciding how they would deal with losing one of their best.

"There's nothing you could have done," Lance said. He was Lance again, and the ghost vowed to be quiet until he could have a word with Alice, if she ever appeared again. "Just give them a little longer. They were both close with her. They need more time before we go back."

"Kevin will be worried," Adrianna said. She was trying not to think about Tiger Lily speared on the ice, or seeing her lying lifeless on the ground with such large holes in her. The images were there whenever she closed her eyes. She wanted to get out of here and far away. "We just disappeared. It's midterms. Someone noticed."

"Don't you worry about that," Arthur told her. "I can make that all go away if you want me to."

"I just have to go out with you again, right?" Her voice was hollow. She was so tired and she wanted this to be over.

"Not this time," he said. "You're much too lovely to be this sad. I'll do this so you can smile again."

"Do you have to be creepy with me right here?" Lance asked.

"You need a teacher, though," Arthur continued. "I don't know how you found one of Merlin's books, but if you're going to learn from them, you'll need someone to show you better control. Throwing things together like you've been doing is dangerous."

"How about we see how Adam's doing?" Lance suggested, bringing her toward the village and the pyre. He shot a sharp look and frown back at Arthur before turning his attention to Adrianna. "Maybe he's ready to go."

Adrianna nodded and went with him, letting her eyes drift to the fire. Peter and Adam sat next to one another in silence and watched the smoke rise into the bright and dark blue sky. That she was so completely gone when she had just been there, Adrianna still didn't know what to think of it.

The gray lifted soon after they put Tiger Lily to rest and something about that seemed wrong. Everything about this felt so wrong. It had happened too quickly, too casually, and caused too much grief. Claudia hadn't even batted an eye at it. Or Morgana. Whatever she was now.

Adam and Peter didn't move when Adrianna came close and she couldn't bring herself to say anything.

Through the flames, Adrianna saw someone else standing on the other side of the pyre. Still in her gym clothes, Alice stared at the flames as if in a trance. Her cheeks shone almost as much as her watering eyes in the flames despite the surrounding daylight, but her expression was empty.

"She's been here a while," Adam said. "We should go back."

Lance let her go and Adrianna dashed around the pyre, catching Alice in a strong hug, pulling her close and tight. It surprised Alice but she didn't fight it, awkwardly returning it as Adrianna let her own tears loose into her shoulder. She'd almost forgotten about Alice and the whole reason they were here. To get her heart back. To keep her from dying. And now look at what they'd done.

But Alice felt warm now, stronger. When she pulled herself away, she didn't look as pale as she did before. There was no sign of the cough building up in her again. Her hands slipped down to grab Alice's wrists, her fingers prodding around until she thought she could feel something there.

"He got it, didn't he?" she asked. She wanted so badly for it to be true. "Cat did it. You have your heart back, don't you?"

Alice nodded, a small smile crossing her lips as she met Adrianna's eyes. "I have my heart back."

Adrianna hugged her tight again. At least it wasn't all bad. At least it wasn't all for nothing.

"We should get back," Adam said.

The others gathered behind Adrianna, just far enough to give them space. Peter didn't look ready to go, his face blank and still staring at the fire, but Adrianna thought it would be best for all of them to leave this place. She nodded and gestured for them all to get closer. "I think I'm getting better at this," she said. She slipped her hand in Alice's. "Come on, let's get out of here."

With a smile on her face, Adrianna gestured wide and they finally left Wonderland. As they did, Alice looked back at the fire, leaving behind her last words for Tiger Lily.

"I'm sorry."

CHAPTER 27

Preparing for Summer

TRUE TO HIS word, Arthur made their disappearance into a non-issue. They could take their midterms and continue with the year as if nothing at all had happened.

But something had happened. Peter was quiet, no longer vibrant like he had been before, and stopped talking to anyone or doing anything he hadn't already agreed to. It concerned Kevin, but he was comfortable giving him some space. He wasn't missing classes, at least.

Likewise, there was a luster lost from Adam as he moved through life as he remained in mourning. He talked to Lance now, at least, and Lance was keeping an eye on him to keep some of his impulses in check. Still, it pained her to see Adam looking so lost, or to see him missing a couple days.

Alice was the only one who seemed to go back to normal. Adrianna watched her more carefully, but she didn't grow tired so easily anymore. She could keep up fine in gym and there was no sign of a cough. When she tried to grab her hand or arm, Alice was always warm under her fingers and she never looked sick. She even stopped wearing makeup to make it easier for Adrianna to tell.

Even better, she continued her new habits instead of going back to her old ones. There was no more disappearing. She still carried books like the rest of them and didn't even vanish to get across campus. She remained social, though perhaps spent a little too much time reading books. She even raised her hand in class now and then still. It was like it was really over.

And she was there when Adrianna needed her. She lost sleep many nights; her dreams turning to nightmares of Wonderland. Alice was quick to wake up and talk Adrianna down, to listen to her every concern and assure her that she wouldn't have to go back. That Alice was safe and she wasn't going back to Wonderland anymore. Alice renewed her promise almost nightly that she wouldn't go back again.

The more time passed, the more that seemed true. Even Lance was back to normal, Adrianna not having seen the ghost showing through since they got back. She had both of her brothers back. It was almost enough to make her stop worrying about where Matt had disappeared to and what might still happen to him over there.

If not for Arthur, she could have forgotten about everything. He was the only one who wanted to bring it back up, insisting he wanted to see the book she had found and telling her it that belonged to his mentor. Telling her that she didn't know how to use it properly. Telling her that he could teach her. If not for Arthur trying to use it to weasel his way into her life, she could just forget about it.

Adrianna was happy that they didn't have to deal with it right now. It might not be completely done yet, and she knew Morgana would come back for Alice again, but for the moment at least there was quiet. There was peace. And for the moment, she could be content that nothing was too wrong. For the moment, all was well.

ALICE TOOK A deep breath as she checked herself over in the mirror. She was still flush from the hot shower and she tied her long blonde hair back into a wet ponytail to keep it out of her face. The days were getting warmer, so her sleeves got shorter in response. She didn't have classes any longer, so a dress seemed appropriate, and no one had thought anything of them. She carefully touched the collar of her shirt, her finger grazing the fine silver chain that hung around her neck.

A knock at the door drew her attention and she looked back. Adrianna wasn't there, at one last Choir practice for the year, and Alice hadn't been expecting company. She left the mirror and opened it and smiled.

"Do you have a minute?" Lance asked.

Alice nodded and moved out of the way to let him in, leaving the door open. He was himself, smiling awkwardly as he made his way in and standing just inside as he glanced back at the door. He took a breath and looked her very carefully over. His hand lifted for only a moment before he let it relax back at his side. "Lancelot thinks you're hiding something."

"And what do you think?"

He looked her over. "I think you're very good at not telling people when something's wrong," he said. "You managed to hide the fact that you didn't have a heart for a long time from everyone. And none of us saw you get it back or put it back. I don't know if you even *can* put your own heart back."

"Well, if you want I can take this dress off for you and you can see for yourself."

She said it very matter of factly, but Lance's eyes still flew open wide at the suggestion. His face flushed a bright red and he quickly turned his eyes away from her, back to the door. "I— I don't— That's—"

Alice watched him, watched the sputtering as he tried to correct himself and maintain even a sliver of composure. He had his hands up, waving her back like she was threatening him, and she tilted her head as she watched, letting the confusion spread into her features and the beating fill her ears. "So curious and yet so scared of the answers. Perhaps if you don't truly want to know, you wouldn't ask."

"I didn't ask!"

"Ah," Alice said, thinking on it only a moment before smiling widely. "I suppose you didn't. But it would be the fastest way to check, now, wouldn't it? Put all that curiosity to rest so you can be less of a cat and more of a boy again."

He wouldn't look at her and inched closer to the door. "You're obviously fine," he said, though none of the redness left his face. "I don't know what he's so worried about. I'm just…"

He gestured and Alice let him go. As soon as he was out, she pressed the door closed and locked it behind him, going back to the mirror and continuing her inspection.

A pair of large purple eyes appeared in the corner, watching her. "More brazen than cunning," the Cheshire Cat mused.

Alice touched the chain around her neck again and drew it up over her head. Sitting at the end of it, tucked so carefully into her shirt, was a small, bright red heart beating in a glass box. It thrummed so much more loudly when she wore it, but as soon as she took it off the beating faded from her ears and she could concentrate again. Gently she ran a thumb over the glass, staring down at it and looking at it carefully.

She needed to wear it now and then. She would stay healthy and alive for as long as she didn't go too long without it. When she wore it, she could hear all of Wonderland, the pain and sorrow as the world was being ripped apart, echoing in her ears. Madness would slip out of her mouth no matter how hard she tried to hold it back. But if she took it off again, her mind was quiet and she would go back to normal, to that version of her that was liked.

But not one who could love. Not that she had been able to make herself before.

She wondered what might have happened if he'd said yes. If she'd taken off everything, if her heart had been in place, if he'd had his way with her, if then she might be able to feel something for him too. Sometimes in the books, that was what it took. Maybe if she just...

"What are you thinking, Alice?" Cat asked.

"If I put it back," she said to no one else, her words quiet as she looked at the necklace. She let it pool in her hands and she opened a small box on her dresser. "If I try harder. If it was anyone." She put the necklace and her heart in the box, closing it. And everything was quiet.

"Perhaps," Cat said. "Perhaps not. Do you remember?"

"Stay away from Wonderland," Alice said. "And if I must, leave my heart behind."

"Only for now."

Alice went back to the collar of her shirt. The hole was smaller now, but it was still there in her chest. Thankfully, no one thought twice about her more conservative clothing choices and she was content to keep the neckline suitably modest. She looked her face over once more, making sure she looked suitably alive and well. She'd have to put her heart on again this evening to keep up the ruse, but it was a ruse worth keeping.

Cat vanished from the mirror and Alice left as well, leaving her heart behind. She grabbed a book, one that was new and exciting, and made her way through the dorms to see her friends one last time before they all had to return home for the summer.

About the Author

TANYA LISLE IS a novelist from Metro Vancouver, British Columbia, who has series littered across genres from supernatural horror to young adult fantasy. She began writing in elementary school, when she started turning homework assignments into short stories and continued this trend well into university. While attending Simon Fraser University, she developed an appreciation for public domain crossovers and cross-platform narratives. She has a shelf full of notebooks with more story ideas than pens lost to the depths of her bag. Now she writes incessantly in hopes of finishing all of them.

Thankfully, her cat, Remy, has figured out how to shut off Tanya's computer when she needs to take a break.

www.ingramcontent.com/pod-product-compliance
Lightning Source LLC
Chambersburg PA
CBHW031052020726
47495CB00007B/1834